From the Files of
Madison Finn

Read all the books about Madison Finn!

#1 Only the Lonely
#2 Boy, Oh Boy!

Coming Soon!

#3 Play It Again

From the Files of

Madison Finn

Boy, Oh Boy!

VOLO
HYPERION
New York

Printed in the United States of America

First Edition
7 9 10 8 6

The main body of text of this book is set in 13-point Frutiger Roman.

ISBN 0-7868-1554-X

Visit www.volobooks.com

For my brother, Andrew MacTaggart,
who is destined for great things

Chapter 1

Fifteen minutes into the start of the school day, and Madison Finn had already chewed off all the orange glitter polish on her left hand. It was one of Madison's thirty or so nervous habits, right up there on the list next to sweating when she tried to play the flute and fleeing the scene when she was embarrassed. She was *very* skilled at fleeing.

Mrs. Wing stood in front of the classroom. "Welcome to the twenty-first century, where technology teacher and librarian morph into one being. Well, online librarian, anyhow. I'm your happy cybrarian, at your service."

"That's *Mrs.* Cybrarian to us, right?" Egg (a.k.a. Walter Diaz) said aloud, his voice warbling.

"Last week we talked about some basic facts about computers," Mrs. Wing said, lecturing from the front of the class. "We covered how hardware is assembled and how chips are made. And Mr. Diaz was kind enough to explain to us how a chip works."

She glanced over to Egg's desk and he grinned a real Grinchy grin.

"No prob', Mrs. Wing," he said.

Madison flared her nostrils. The only thing she hated more than Egg's constant crushing on teachers was when he was being extra cocky. Ever since Madison and Egg were kids, he had crushed on pretty female teachers. First it was kindergarten's Miss Jeremiah; now it was the seventh-grade cybrarian.

Mrs. Wing fit into Egg's crush category perfectly. She was prettier than pretty, Madison thought. Her long hair was swept up into a French twist and she wore a long plum-colored skirt, a neat white blouse, and a red bead necklace. She moved around the room as if she were walking on cotton balls, floating from computer station to station, beads *plink-plink-plinking* together.

"Now, what I'd like to try out with the class this week are some basic programming skills," Mrs. Wing continued. "I think we're all ready to move ahead, am I right?"

Lance, a quiet kid who always sat at the back of the classroom, raised his hand and shook his head,

dejected. He didn't get computers and felt *way* left out. He was *not* ready. Not by a long jump. Or was it a shot put?

Madison shot Egg a glance, but, thankfully, Mrs. Wing said she'd explain it again *later*.

"Learning Basic," Mrs. Wing went on, "means that every one of you in this room will be able to program a computer. Just think about that. Think about what that could do for all of you. And looking around, I can see already that I have a classroom filled with technological geniuses . . . even *you*, Lance."

As soon as she said that, someone on the other side of the room snorted. Madison realized it was Egg's best friend, Drew Maxwell, who laughed when he heard the words *Lance* and *genius* uttered in the same breath. And as soon as he snorted, Egg snorted too. And then this kid P.J. Rigby snorted. And then Jason Szelewski, Beth Dunfey, Suresh Dhir—*every-one* snorted.

It sounded like a pig farm.

Mrs. Wing didn't get mad, though. She just sort of snorted right back.

"Well, I can see we'll be having a lot of fun in here, class. Just let's make sure it's not at someone *else's* expense, okay?"

Madison saw Egg making puppy-dog eyes at the back of Mrs. Wing's head when she said that. Turning away, Madison reread her onscreen notes.

```
Dim strTemper As String
Const strNormNumbers$ = "0123456789"
Exit Function
End If
End If
OnlyNumericTextInput = strSource
End Function
```

After reviewing her page of code about strings and substrings and lots of little dollar signs, Madison popped in a disk and booted up her own personal file.

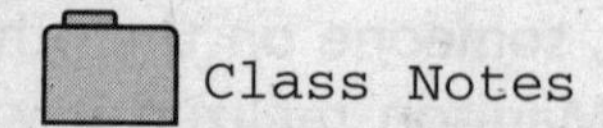

Class Notes

Nothing at Far Hills Junior High is what I expected. I thought it would be way different than middle school. NOT. I figured there was no way the same people from Far Hills Elementary would be geeks or popular but that is just the way it is, like the same thing as last year but in a different building. Dad says I always overthink this kind of stuff but it's just so hard to hold back a thought sometimes.

Mrs. Wing is sooo smart, so she probably will catch me right now writing personal stuff, and not school stuff but oh well. She's all the way on the other side of the room.

I like the way her beads look like red jelly beans. I wear a ring on almost every

single finger, but I don't go for necklaces so much. Maybe I should?

Something about seventh grade was inspiring Madison. With a new laptop and a brand-new scanner, maybe she could become a techno-queen for a change.

"She's so cool, right?" Egg nudged Madison and stared as Mrs. Wing flew around to the other side of the classroom.

"Egg," Madison whispered back. "Aren't you bored? We know this stuff already."

"Bored? Not me," Egg replied, pie-eyed. "Why ask for more work? Are you crazy, Maddie? You want *more* work?"

Madison sneered. "Gimme a break. Egg, don't you want to learn something new?"

"Learn? Geesh, you sound like my mom," Egg's pal Drew butted in.

"Yeah, Maddie," Egg said, copying him. "You sound like *my* mom, too."

"Yeah, Maddie," Drew said again.

"Hey, quit it!" Madison snapped.

The two boys laughed and high-fived each other softly.

"At least I don't have a crush on someone who reminds me of my mom," Madison said, looking in Mrs. Wing's direction. She crossed her arms in front of her chest, daring him to respond.

"Put a lid on it, guys," Drew suddenly warned, yanking Egg's fleece.

Mrs. Wing was headed back toward their computer stations.

"Mr. Diaz. Miss Finn. Problem here?" Mrs. Wing said.

Madison and Egg looked at their monitors and grunted at the same time in the same monotone. "No, Mrs. Wing. No problem."

Then she looked over at Drew.

He tried not to react. But it's hard to hold back a snort.

"Do I need to separate you three?" Mrs. Wing said, tapping her foot. Madison thought she would stay like that forever, huffing and puffing and looking disappointed, but in less than a minute she gave up. Mrs. Wing had to help Lance, who was lost in Basic again.

Madison glared at Drew and Egg. "Don't get me in trouble, guys!"

"Maddie, you are a stress puppy," Egg said. Drew nodded in agreement.

Madison gave them both another nasty look and they all went back to their computer screens.

Of course Madison was overly sensitive these days to begin with. She missed her parents.

Dad was out of town on business, all the way across the country. He was meeting with the design firm that had helped set up his Web site. He was launching a new business *again*. Madison couldn't remember what exactly it was going to be.

Mom was also gone. She'd left yesterday to head overseas on a business trip for Budge Films, a movie production company that made small nature documentaries. During the summer, Madison had been able to travel along with her mom on another journey—to South America—to film rare tree frogs. But there was no more traveling allowed together now, not during *school days*.

Mom always said, "You have more important things to take care of during the school year, Maddie. Like getting your junior high diploma."

So while Mom was meeting with lots of French people and eating plates of *pommes frites*, Madison stayed put in Far Hills. She and her dog, Phin, were camped out for the duration at Aimee's house.

Staying at Aimee's was a treat. Aimee Anne Gillespie wasn't just Madison Francesca Finn's best friend. Madison liked to think of her as a sister. They had known each other since birth.

"Um, Mrs. Wing? Could you help me out with this?" Egg was mooning in the teacher's direction again. Madison wanted to gag. He may have acted all tough and smart, but in computer class Egg was *definitely* soft-boiled.

While the rest of the class continued working on their Basic assignment, Madison tried to sneak on line. The system connected, but she couldn't get on to her favorite site, bigfishbowl.com.

```
No Access! See your Cybrarian!
```

On these classroom computers, there were built-in blocks preventing students from online access except at designated times. Madison knew Mrs. Wing had put up all the blocks. She knew how to keep everyone focused on the assignment and only the assignment—didn't she?

This was going to be a long week.

Madison could feel the low dull ache that burns inside when you really, *really* miss someone.

And it wasn't just Mom or Dad.

Madison missed her purple blow-up chair, her file cabinet, her miles of files, and all her other *stuff*. Madison missed the way her bare feet felt on Mom's wood floors and the way the kitchen table rocked on one side when you leaned on it. She missed the way her pug Phinnie liked to curl up in front of the dishwasher during the dry cycle.

Right now, thinking about it too much, Madison missed everything about home. Or at least about the way home had used to be, when Mom and Dad were still together.

"Psssst!" Drew suddenly whispered over to Madison. "Are you having trouble getting online?"

Madison nodded. She was having *all* kinds of trouble. But she was glad to know she wasn't the only one bored with the assignment.

"I know a secret back entrance," he said, still

whispering so Mrs. Wing couldn't hear. "I can tell you the secret password that only the teachers are supposed to know."

"Oh really? Then how do you—?"

Madison dropped her head down a little because Mrs. Wing was slowly making her way over to their desks.

Brrrrrrrring.

The cybrarian code would have to be cracked later.

"And we are outta here!" Madison's brain whirred as she zipped up her orange backpack.

"Uh, Madison Finn, could you hold on a moment?" Mrs. Wing held up her hand for Madison to wait around. Everyone else who was still in the room stopped and stared.

"Oooo, you're in trouble now!" Egg whispered.

"Oh, shut up," Madison grunted under her breath. She scratched her cheek. It was so hot. Everything was happening in slo-mo.

"Later for you, Maddie." Egg was ready to walk out.

"Want us to hang outside?" Drew said to Madison. "I mean, we can wait here in the hall."

Egg was getting impatient. "Come on, Drew-fus. Let's make like a tree—"

"Don't leave!" Madison buzzed. "What do you guys think she wants? Do you think she knows I was trying to get online? I mean, I know I shouldn't have

been working on my own disk in class, but do you guys think—"

Madison had never *ever* been asked to stay after class. And she had never ever *ever* been asked to do it in front of a whole bunch of kids either, let alone ones who didn't know her. It was the worst moment of seventh grade so far. Madison was panicked.

Drew shrugged. "Maddie, it's probably nothing."

Egg looked over at Mrs. Wing. "I wish she was keeping *me* after class."

Oh boy.

Chapter 2

Madison slumped into a blue chair near Mrs. Wing's desk.

She felt blue, too.

"Madison, I noticed you seemed a little distracted in class," Mrs. Wing began.

"Distracted?" Madison repeated with concern. She gazed over Mrs. Wing's head so she wouldn't have to look her in the eye. As usual, she expected the worst kind of news.

"Well, you seem bored," she said, beads clacking again.

Madison frowned. "I do?"

"And I don't like seeing that," Mrs. Wing continued.

Madison sighed.

"Well, why would I? You are obviously good at computers. And I'm your teacher. I want to keep you challenged. Not bored."

Madison tilted her head to the side. "You do?"

"Of course," Mrs. Wing chuckled, which broke the tension a little. She sat on the edge of her old metal desk. "I want this to be your favorite class, of course. Isn't that what all teachers are supposed to say?"

Madison smiled. "But this is my favorite class. And I am not just saying that. Really. Truly."

"Madison, are you interested in doing something special with the Computer Center this year? Usually I ask eighth graders to do this—"

"Something special?"

"Class elections are coming up and I'm the faculty advisor. I am responsible for getting the elections up and running on the Web. The school wants your classmates to vote online for the very first time this year. Far Hills just got a brand-new proxy server over the summer!"

"Proxy *wha*?" Madison asked.

"Server. It's a computer that will support our own special network right here in the building. And what I need is someone to help me to maintain the site—download photos, results, and other new information on a regular basis. Then we will have everyone in seventh grade vote online."

Madison didn't know what to say.

Mrs. Wing just grinned. "So, Madison, what's the verdict? Would you be interested in helping out?"

Madison nodded, but no words came out.

"I take that as a yes?" Mrs. Wing joked.

"Yes!" Madison said at last.

"As you know, we have less than two weeks until the election, so I will need you to stay after school to work on the site, answer e-mails, and other work. We can talk specifics tomorrow. Does that sound like something you might be able to do?"

Madison nodded with delight. She felt as if someone had just handed her a winning Lotto ticket. She really could be techno-queen.

"So." Mrs. Wing held out her hand to shake. "Are we a team then?"

"Yessss!" Madison gushed again. She grabbed her backpack and started for the door. "I can't believe this, Mrs. Wing. I can't. I swear I will be the best, best, best Web-site person ever."

Mrs. Wing laughed. "I'm sure you will be. See you tomorrow."

On her way out of the room, Madison's mind turned to mush. She had never been asked to do something like this by a teacher before.

"What did she say?" Egg said, leaping out from a bank of lockers.

Madison jumped. "Oh, Egg you scared me—"

"We were waiting for you all this time," Egg said. "Spill it."

The first bell was ringing. Aimee and Fiona walked up to the lockers.

Fiona Waters was Madison's newest best friend from over the summer. She and her family, including twin brother Chet, had moved to Far Hills from California. Even though she was a little bit spacey, Madison liked Fiona a lot.

"Hey, Maddie," Fiona said, "what's going on? Were you just in computer?"

"Yes, she was," Egg chimed in. "And Mrs. Wing kept her after class. She was about to tell me."

Madison scowled at Egg. "What is your problem?"

"Hey, Walter," Fiona said coyly. Of course Egg was too busy bugging Madison to give Fiona a hello or even a smile.

"Did you say 'Walter'?" Aimee asked, shaking her head. She laughed. "Fiona, his name is Egg. Nobody calls him Walter except his mother."

Fiona looked a little embarrassed.

"Maddie, are you gonna tell me or *what*?" Egg asked again.

"Well, gimme a chance, all right?"

Madison was busting to tell Egg and everyone else what Mrs. Wing had said to her after class. But everyone else wouldn't shut up.

"Hold it!" Aimee said. "Is this because something happened in computer class?"

"Is everything okay? Did you get into trouble?" asked Drew.

"Why won't you just tell us?" Egg yelled again.

"I am TRYING!" Madison yelled and then quickly lowered her voice. "I am trying to tell you but you guys keep talking. Okay. What happened is that Mrs. Wing says she wants *me* to help her run all of the online elections for Far Hills Junior High. That's it."

"She *what*?" Egg wasn't smiling.

"Hey, that's pretty cool," Drew said.

Madison continued, "She wants me to be Election Web Manager or something like that for the school Web site."

"You?" Egg slapped his forehead.

"Yeah, *me*. What's wrong with that?"

"What about *me*?" Egg said.

"You can't have everything your way, Egg," Aimee snapped.

"That is so awesome, Maddie!" Fiona chimed in.

"Yeah, way to go," Drew added.

Aimee grinned. "Maddie, you will totally be the best person for the job."

Egg backed himself up against a bank of lockers. "But I am the one who taught you how to go online, Madison. It should be me who gets this, not you!"

"Egg, just chill out," Aimee said. "It is no big deal."

"It is a deal," Egg said. "This is a big, fat, *hairy* deal."

"I'm sorry, Egg." Madison stood there for a moment waiting for Egg to say something else, but he didn't.

The second bell rang, echoing in the hall.

"Look, you guys, I gotta run!" Drew waved as he wandered away. "Got a class . . ."

"See ya, Drew." Madison waved back. "Egg?"

Egg was already walking in the other direction.

"What a pain," Aimee said.

Madison hated the fact that Egg was annoyed, but she also knew that no matter what was said right now, tomorrow he would get over it and they'd be friends just as before. She hoped.

As she, Aimee, and Fiona moved off toward their next class, a voice called out from near the water fountain.

"Hey, Finnster!"

Finnster was a nickname Hart Jones had called Madison way back when they had been in first grade. It was a dorky name and she hated it, but he did it anyway. After second grade, Hart had moved away, but now he was back and the name was back, too.

Aimee chuckled under her breath. She elbowed

Madison in the side. "Hey, I think he likes you."

Fiona was giggling.

"Hart?" Madison groaned. "Get real."

"Just like a fairy tale," Aimee laughed. "Once he was a frog and now he's a prince."

"Ribbit." Fiona laughed some more.

Madison walked faster. She heard Hart call out again, "Hey, Finnster!" but breezed on by pretending not to hear.

Aimee and Fiona heard and responded at the exact same time, however.

"Hi, Hart. 'Bye, Hart."

"Isn't Hart cousins with Drew?" Fiona asked Aimee as they walked away.

"You know he really has gotten sooooo cute." Aimee teased Madison some more.

"And he's really tall for a seventh grader."

"Yeah, whatever," Madison moaned. "I don't hang out with him anymore."

"Maybe you should," Fiona said.

"No thank you very much," Madison replied.

"I forgot you think all boys are just idiots," Aimee said.

Fiona laughed. "Maybe that's true. I know my brother Chet is."

Aimee stopped and grabbed one of Madison's hands. "Maddie, what are you gonna do if this boy really does like you? What then?" She looked down at Madison's fingers. "Hey, what happened to the

nail polish I put on last week? It's all chewed off."

"Oh, that," Madison said, glancing down at whatever was left of the glitter polish. "It was delicious," she said walking toward study hall.

 Boys

Is something wrong with me? I cannot believe the way life works these days. I spend all summer stressing out about being a seventh grader. Now that I'm here I am just stressing out about something else.

Is Egg right? Am I a total stress puppy? No wait, my dog, Phinnie, is the stress puppy. I'm the stress *person*.
Ha ha.

I'm just not like Aimee or Fiona. I just don't see the point in wasting time trying to get some stupid boy to like me. Every time Aimee likes someone she always changes her mind anyhow. It's not real. I don't want to pretend. I want the real thing when I have it. I would rather just stay friends anyway. That is easier.

Aimee doesn't even know what it's like because she always can talk to boys. And Fiona is good at flirting too, even if Egg is the one she flirts with.

NO BOYS FOR ME.

I have to worry about other stuff like

the election Web site and not boys. I have to make sure the school election is the best ever. Mrs. Wing is counting on me.

Madison spent the entire study hall period working at the lone computer station up in the library. Students were allowed to work in the classroom, the library, or the media center. Madison liked to escape to the top floor of the school's main building whenever she could. It seemed like no one else ever came up here, so Madison had it scoped out as *her* secret place—a place where she could go to hide, think, do homework, and even update her files. Mr. Books, the librarian, knew Madison by sight, since she came up at least twice a week.

After study hall, Madison wandered into the newspaper office to pick up some photos and bios of class presidential candidates. It was for the Web site, of course. This was Mrs. Wing's first "official" assignment for her.

Madison loved the way the newspaper room smelled like ink and glue and copy paper. Maybe she should try out for the newspaper staff? Madison was having trouble figuring out which after-school activities were the most important. She loved the computer, but Madison wanted to try other things, too.

There on the desk at the front of the room was a rubber-banded pile of envelopes with a simple note: "For Mrs. Wing: 7th-grade candidates."

Madison picked up the envelopes.

In envelope number one was a photo of Madison's enemy number one, Ivy Daly, also known as Poison Ivy. Madison had been calling her that for a few years now, ever since they had their major falling-out in third grade.

So far, Ivy was the only girl at Far Hills Junior High running for class president. She was going to win. Everyone knew Ivy.

For one thing, Ivy was pretty smart.

For another thing, she was pretty pretty.

Ivy was also wicked good at talking to boys. She was even better at it than Aimee, which was saying a lot. With those talents, how could she lose a seventh-grade election?

Ivy also surrounded herself with influential supporters like Roseanne Snyder and Joan Kenyon. They were two drones who stuck to Ivy like superglue and made fun of all the people who weren't just like them. Rose and Joan were intimidating even when they didn't speak. Madison knew deep down they were fakers. She called them Rose *Thorn* and *Phony* Joanie behind their backs. But even if they were obnoxious, they would still help Ivy win. Safety in numbers.

As she stared at Ivy, Madison got less excited about her new Web assignment.

At first it seemed so exciting, being picked to be in charge of the election site. Madison could be the

boss for once. But now, looking at Ivy, Madison felt discouraged.

How could she enjoy any election when she *hated* the number one candidate?

Chapter 3

"Miss Finn, you'll be working with Miss Daly."

In science class, Mr. Danehy was assigning lab partners.

Madison got Poison Ivy.

"So is it true that you're like in charge of the election?" Ivy asked as they paired off together and sat on their stools at the lab counter.

"It's true," Madison mumbled, trying to say as little as possible.

"I heard from Mrs. Wing that you're the one doing the school Web site or something."

News travels fast around junior high, Madison thought, pasting on her best plastic smile. "Yes, I am in charge of the Web site. Mrs. Wing asked me."

"Oh," Ivy said with a perplexed look on her face.

"Why should you care, Ivy?"

"Care?" Ivy said. "Because I am only like the number-one candidate for seventh-grade president. Like, where have you been? Didn't you see my posters in the cafeteria?"

Madison pretended like she'd swallowed something the wrong way and cleared her throat. Ivy kept talking.

"So far it's just me and Montrell Morris and Tommy Kwong. Should be an easy election, really."

Madison stared down at the lab's black countertop, feeling like she'd been drop-kicked. Everything seemed so rosy first period. Now she had gone from being singled out by Mrs. Wing to being *bummed* out by Poison Ivy. What fun would it be working on an election when the enemy had the distinct advantage?

"You *are* gonna vote for me, right?" Ivy said.

"Well," Madison said, gritting her teeth. "I'm not sure who I'm voting for yet."

"Whatever," Ivy said, opening her science book.

The clock said 11:22. Could Madison make it through the other forty-eight minutes until science class ended?

She wasn't so sure.

Right now Madison Finn wanted to slam her science teacher Mr. Danehy for putting her in this position, at this table, with Ivy Daly. She would have preferred being matched up with *anyone* else on the planet. Even Hart Jones would have been an okay lab partner.

Madison looked across the class at Hart. He and Fiona's twin brother, Chet, had been paired off together. They were becoming fast friends, Madison could tell by the way they goofed around. Madison looked at Hart's hair, combed back off his face. His black glasses were slipping down his nose and he looked nerdy, but he also looked cute.

Was he really the same Hart Jones who used to chase her around at recess and try to pull her hair? Madison suddenly realized she was staring.

"And one more thing! You will *NOT* leave science lab early under any conditions," Mr. Danehy's voice boomed. "If you and your partner finish up an assignment, simply move along to the extra-credit questions. I do not encourage loafing, is that clear? This is not a place to have conversations, this is a place to learn science. Clear?"

Mr. Danehy had set up microscopes all over the room. Lab partners were asked to record their simple observations as they viewed a series of slides.

Of course, Ivy didn't feel like looking. "I'll just copy your answers?" she said to Madison. "After all, we are partners, right?"

Madison bit her lip. She looked into the microscope and adjusted the magnification knob.

"What you are looking at right now," Mr. Danehy said, "is a slide of human spit."

A couple of girls and guys said, "Eeeeeew" but then leaned in to get a closer look. Madison took a

look, too, while Ivy drummed her fingers against the lab table, impatient.

"This is so stupid. Spit? Gimme a break. What about cells or something a little more scientific?"

Madison pushed the microscope toward Ivy. "Why don't you see for yourself? There's science going on there. Science like *cells*, you know."

Ivy scoffed. "I don't think so. Get that spit away from me."

Madison ignored Ivy and looked into the microscope. She adjusted it once again for the next slide.

Ivy jumped off her stool and walked to the front of the classroom. She needed a hall pass to use the bathroom. She said she had to pee, but Madison suspected she was going in there a) to apply more lip gloss; b) to make a call on her cell phone (a little pink phone she carried everywhere); or c) to get away from the spit slide once and for all.

Mr. Danehy handed Ivy a hall pass and then disappeared into the science closet. Once he was gone, everyone started talking and moving around. Hart Jones wandered over to Madison's table.

"Hey, there," he said gruffly.

Madison rolled her eyes but didn't speak.

"Uh, I seem to have lost my fruit fly. Have you seen him?"

Madison was mortified. Was anyone else listening? She couldn't help but laugh a little bit at Hart's

stupid attempt at a joke, but she certainly didn't want anyone else to hear it.

Hart cracked another joke about someone's fruit fly being open.

Madison laughed a little more. She liked the way his hair twisted on top of his head. This was the first time she'd ever noticed that he had a cowlick. It looked like a wave of dark chocolate. She wondered why he had come over to talk to her. Why was he just standing there making jokes?

Mr. Danehy pulled out a large container from the closet. It was filled with hundreds of *living* fruit flies. Quickly, he dropped in a cotton ball with chloroform. In two minutes all the flies were knocked out. Chet yelled out, "Fruit flies dead! Details at eleven!" Everyone laughed.

When Mr. Danehy was almost done showing the flies to the room, Ivy walked back in. She walked in just in time to watch Hart slip off her stool and make his way back to his own seat as the class settled down.

"Did I miss much?" Ivy said, eyeing Hart and Chet across the room, and pushing Madison to the side a little bit so she could squeeze back into her chair.

Madison grabbed at the counter edge, but she lost her balance. She fell forward, knocking into a cardboard tray of glass beakers.

Crash.

"What did you do that for?" Ivy screeched. "I can't believe you!"

The beaker of stunned flies survived. Unfortunately, Madison's pride did not.

Mr. Danehy rushed over. "Nobody move. I'm gonna sweep up this mess. Watch the glass, girls."

From across the room, Hart yelled out, "Way to go, Finnster!"

Madison turned beet purple as the class laughed.

"Finnster?" Ivy laughed. "Nice name, Madison. For a circus act, maybe."

The last thing Madison wanted to do was to call attention to herself, and yet here she was, the center of the chaos. Everyone was staring and laughing. Ivy was pointing. And Hart was calling her Finnster.

She couldn't believe it.

"Miss Finn, Miss Daly," Mr. Danehy said as he plucked up the glass shards. "This is absolutely not your fault—"

"Well, I *KNOW* it's not *my* fault," Ivy interrupted.

"I should not have had the containers here . . ."

"Oh, well, Madison probably didn't mean to make a big mess," Ivy said. "I mean I tried to grab the materials for her but she fell off the chair—"

Madison's jaw dropped.

"Madison, you really have to be careful in science class," Ivy went on, smirking. Mr. Danehy believed every word.

He patted her on the back. "Well, it's no problem,

Madison. We all make mistakes and get caught off balance, don't we?"

All at once, Madison felt tears coming but she sucked on her top front teeth, inhaled deep, and held them in. She wanted to flee—*badly*.

If Ivy Daly did not shut her trap in T-minus-30 seconds, Madison was ready to do the fifty-yard dash down the hall. She tried to hold on.

By the time science class finally ended, Madison's stomach ached from holding on so long. She watched as Ivy, Rose, and Joanie exited class at the exact same time as Hart and Chet.

"Aren't you Bart Jones?" Ivy said, tossing her hair.

Chet grunted. "Who wants to know?"

Hart just smiled. "Yeah, I'm Hart Jones. With an H."

Madison could hear every word.

Ivy tossed her hair again. "Oh yeah, H for Hart. Do you remember me?" She cocked her hip to the side and twirled a strand of her red hair. Her jeans were cut low on her waist so that Madison could almost see her belly button.

Madison wasn't sure why, but she didn't want to see Hart with Poison Ivy. As they were standing there, Hart turned around once and caught Madison's eye. But then he looked away again.

"Madison!" Mr. Danehy said loudly.

"What?" Madison said, stunned.

"Don't forget your books."

Madison grabbed them and pushed her way over to the door. For a brief moment, she was stuck right between Ivy and Hart.

"Excuuuuuse me." She nudged Ivy and walked through.

Ivy clucked her tongue. "Way to be pushy, Madison."

Hart stared at the floor.

On the way home, Madison talked with Aimee and Fiona about the day's events: the good, the bad, and the ugly. The good news about the election Web site, the bad news about the tiff with Egg, and the ugly—Poison Ivy Daly.

"*OH MY GOD*, she can *NOT* win this election!" Aimee exclaimed. "She is such a kiss-up."

"Who else is running?" Fiona asked. "Is that Montrell guy?"

"Yeah, Montrell Morris. He's funny."

"And Tommy Kwong, too," Madison added. "He's one of the leads in Drama Club."

"Ivy Daly *MUST* not win," Aimee said again with emphasis.

Fiona nodded. "I really didn't think she was so bad at first, but I really see what you mean about her being a little too—"

"Two-faced?" Aimee shouted.

"Yeah, well, if you put it that way, I have to agree," Fiona joked.

"Did you guys see the way she was acting in school assembly last week?" Aimee pointed out. "She was kissing up to Principal Bernard after he made another one of his stupid speeches." Aimee moaned, doing her best Ivy imitation. "Ooooh, Mr. Bernard, you're sooooo funny!"

"She's disgusting when she hangs all over the teachers. That's how she is in science, too. She was even flirting with Hart Jones today."

"Hart?" Aimee screeched. *"NO WAY!"* Aimee, as usual, was being a little dramatic.

"Yeah," Madison groaned. "And Ivy was doing that thing she always does. That guy thing."

Fiona asked, "What *guy* thing?"

"Hey, *do* you like Hart or something?" Aimee said.

Madison blushed. "No."

"You do like him!" Fiona screeched. "Look at you!"

"I do *NOT* like Hart Jones. Will you guys just stop, already." Madison sighed.

Aimee started back in on the subject of their least favorite classmate. "You know, for once I wish things would not go Ivy's way."

"She's eviler than evil," Madison said.

"I don't think any of us will be signing up for an Ivy for President fan club," Aimee said.

"Not me," Madison agreed.

"Well then, me neither," said Fiona.

If there had ever been any doubt at the start of seventh grade about what new kids were friends with what old kids, that doubt ended here. Fiona was with Madison and Aimee all the way.

Continuing up the street, Madison felt the quick breeze in the air that announced fall was really on its way. Gone were the afternoons of running through freshly cut lawns and sprinklers and all things summer. The sky was getting dark earlier now. Gone were the sidewalk smells of lilacs and honeysuckle, replaced by the sweet scent of firewood and damp, cool air. Soon all the trees in the neighborhood would blend yellow, red, and *orange*—Madison's favorite color in the whole world. Maybe the breezes could blow away all the bad vibes of school?

Madison hoped so.

"So does Egg have a girlfriend?" Fiona said all of a sudden, switching to a new subject.

"Egg?" Madison laughed.

Aimee stopped short.

"He really is a cutie," Fiona said shyly. "I know I said that before but—"

"Fiona Waters, did you just say Egg was *CUTE*?" Aimee laughed out loud.

"Don't you think so?" Fiona said. "I don't know why but he is just so—"

"Are you nuts?" Aimee asked seriously. "No, Fiona, I mean it. *ARE YOU NUTS*?"

"Noooo." Fiona grinned. She was a little

embarrassed, but she didn't stop talking about it. "I just think he's cute."

Aimee doubled over with laughter. Madison had to hold back her own attack of the giggles, too. How could someone *really* like Egg, the same Egg who had burped "Yankee Doodle" at field day last year?

Aimee and Madison were practically keeling over in hysterics, but Fiona wasn't going back on what she had said.

"Go ahead and laugh," Fiona said. "Whatever."

"We're not laughing at you, I swear," Madison said.

"You really have boys on the brain, don't you?" Aimee smiled.

"Don't you?" Fiona asked.

Fiona didn't get a chance to hear their answers. From across the front lawn where the girls were standing, someone suddenly howled.

"Fi-moan-a, you're *LATE*!"

It was Fiona's twin brother Chet.

Fiona yelled back, "Coming!" and looked down at her silver watch. "Oh! I am soooo busted! Tonight is my Dad's birthday and I gotta make a cake and Mom's gonna—'bye!"

She dashed across the lawn.

Madison tried to say, "Wanna walk to school tomor—?" but it was too late.

Fiona was already inside the house.

Chapter 4

As Madison walked inside Aimee's house, Phineas T. Phin, Madison's snuggly pug, rushed the front door.

"Phinnie!" Madison squealed, chasing him into the family room. His little pug tail squiggled. He was allowed to stay at the Gillespie house too when Mom was away because he could hang out with Aimee's dog, Blossom, a sad-looking girl basset hound with bloodshot eyes.

Her arms full, Madison chased Phinnie into the next room to get his personalized dish, which said PHIN FOOD on the side.

"Whoa, there!" Roger jumped back. "You're about to crash into me!"

Roger was the oldest child in Aimee's family. At twenty-three, he was busy helping Mr. Gillespie with

The Book Web, the family bookstore, while he saved up money for graduate school. He had thick blond hair like his sister. Madison liked the way it waved. He was really smart and talented.

Older brothers were so great. Aimee was so lucky. She had *four* of them.

"Hey, Ma says keep it down in here you guys and, oh yeah, dinner is in like an hour," said another one of Aimee's brothers, Billy, coming into the room. The soles of his sneakers were peeled back to reveal ratty yellow socks. He was an undecided sophomore at Briarwood, the local community college. Billy couldn't decide what TV show to watch, let alone decide on a major or minor.

He clicked past ten channels, which annoyed Aimee.

"Billy, don't be a jerko," she yelled, looking disgusted. "You are such a—"

"Bonehead, just give sis the remote." Roger flicked a finger on the back of Billy's head.

"No way," he responded. "Quit poking me."

Roger poked him again. The two brothers started a slap fight.

Aimee, as usual, was not amused.

"Roger! Billy! Can't you be a little bit more normal? What is your problem?" Aimee's voice increased in volume with each word. "Maddie, let's go up to my room before dinner. My stupid brothers are soooooo embarrassing."

Madison picked up her bag and laptop computer case, followed closely behind by panting Phin and Blossom. She caught one last look at Roger and Billy, sprawled across the couch as she left the room. Aimee had her brothers all wrong. These boys seemed perfect.

Half an hour later, everyone was gathered together again at the Gillespie dinner table for a health food feast.

This is a long way from one of Mom's Scary Dinners, Madison thought as she and Aimee silently devoured their platefuls of delicious homemade spaghetti and tofu meatballs. Madison hoped chewing quickly would help make the tofu taste more like real meatballs. Healthy dinners could *also* be scary ones in their own way.

The boys chattered and chewed and burped, seated in an arc around one side of the table. Madison caught herself staring a few times. She hoped no one else caught her doing it. It was like a piece of her brain had become fixated on boys, even boys who were Aimee's brothers.

She didn't know why. It just was just one of those things.

Before they got ready for bed, Madison found a little downtime to go online. She hadn't been on her computer since yesterday.

FROM	SUBJECT
✉ BUSTER	Sk8ing Message for You
✉ finnrpalzyfg_gogo	Earn $$$ at Home
✉ ff_BUDGEFILM	bonjour!
✉ BUSTER	Sk8ing Message for You

Dad always warned Madison about opening unexpected e-mails and attachments in her mailbox. Tonight she deleted them without even opening the files. She figured the BUSTER Special Message was some kind of advertisement and she wasn't interested in "earning $$$ at home."

That left one *real* message.

Getting Mom's e-mail tonight was like getting tucked in via long distance.

From: ff_BUDGEFILM
To: MadFinn
Subject: bonjour!
Date: Mon 11 Sept 2:06 PM

Bonjour mon amour! Comment va l'ecole? I love you so much, sweetheart, and I miss you already! I thought you might have fun figuring out the little bit of French here.

The weather over here is rain,

rain, rain. Have to get me a new parapluie. That's umbrella, by the way. We're on site all week but I promise to write and call. You must be having fun with Aimee.

Au revoir!
Love you, Mom

ff_BUDGEFILM

Ms. Francine Finn
Vice President of Research and Development
Senior Producer
Budge Films, Inc.

"Hey, can we turn out the lights, Maddie?" Aimee grumbled in a sleepy voice. She put down her copy of *The Outsiders* and rolled over. "Good night."

It was getting later than late. The clock said 10:25 P.M. Madison punched a few keys to save Mom's message and then typed one last e-mail, a note to her brand-new keypal, Bigwheels, whom she had met in a special chat room on bigfishbowl.com. Bigwheels was starting seventh grade too.

From: MadFinn
To: Bigwheels
Subject: School elections and stuff
Date: Mon 11 Sept 10:32 PM

Sorry FTBOMBH that I haven't written! Well, I actually cannot believe a week has passed. How r u???? School is getting to be a little bit weird. I should have written sooner. HELP!

We're in the middle of school elections right now and it feels like total chaos. I'm not running for president or class rep or anything but I am in the middle of it all. I feel like I am ALWAYS in the middle of SOMETHING!

The computer teacher asked me to help her put all the school elections onto the computer and I'm soooo nervous. What if I make a mistake?

Actually, I wonder sometimes what's the point of the whole thing. It's all decided already. Did I mention that my sworn enemy is probably gonna win and rule the school? I just don't know what magic power she has over everyone so they like her, but they do. How come the people you like the least end up being around you the most? And the

people you love the most go away when you need them? It's a drag.

All I can say is TAL, PAL! Just for being out there in the Web world. I feel not so alone just writing now.

Oh—I have 1 more very important question!!! Is it possible to suddenly like someone when you didn't like him AT ALL yesterday?

Do you have a boyfriend?
Yeah, I know that was two questions.
Yours till the nail tips,
MadFinn

After she sent the message, Madison yanked on her favorite GRRRILLA POWER T-shirt with the ape on the front and crawled silently into Aimee's trundle bed. She loved the way the sheets smelled like cinnamon at Aimee's house.

Once again that creepy yellow hall light clicked on, casting an eerie glow that danced and bobbed along Aimee's wall. Madison thought for a moment how funny it was that *everything* in Aimee's world—even the shadows of her bedroom—danced.

Aimee's room was so quiet Madison could hear herself blink.

"Maddie?" Aimee whispered from under the covers.

Night vision kicked in as Madison rolled over on her side to see her friend's face. "Yeah?"

"I can't sleep."

"Sorry."

"No, I've been thinking about our conversations today. You know, about Ivy and all."

"Yeah?"

"Why do you think we want her to lose so badly?"

Madison shrugged but then realized, of course, Aimee couldn't see her in the dark. "I dunno. Because we do. Because we want to see her lose, for once."

"Because sometimes, I dunno. I feel bad about being so nasty. Like I'm so mean or something—"

"Well, you're *NOT*," Madison said. "And neither am I. She had her chance to be our friend, and she totally blew it."

"Ivy always gets her way, doesn't she? She always wins."

"Yeah." Madison yawned. She was getting a little sleepy, but she made herself stay awake to talk some more. "Well, she won't win this time."

"She's the only girl running, Maddie. Of course she'll win."

Madison yawned again. "Yeah, I guess."

"I just wish we could get back at her in some way. Not like revenge. Just something to show her that—"

"To show her that she is not the queen of the universe?"

"Exactly."

Madison scrunched her toes up under the covers. It was cold in Aimee's room.

"Maddie, I think I know. I have an idea.

"Tell me," Madison whispered. "Just say it."

"I think that the way to get back at Ivy for everything she's ever done to us," Aimee said softly, white teeth flashing a sudden smile in the dark, "is to make sure she has some *real* competition in the election.

"Yeah," Madison agreed, "I guess Montrell Morris and Tommy Kwong don't have a chance."

"Like you said, they're gonna split the boy vote."

Madison wondered aloud, "Too bad there isn't a way to split up the girl vote, too."

"There is. I'm gonna run against her," Aimee said matter-of-factly.

"You're what?" Madison propped herself up onto one elbow.

Aimee sat up in bed and clicked on the lamp on her nightstand. Madison squinted.

"I'm gonna run against Poison Ivy in this class president election," Aimee said with growing confidence. "And I'm gonna win."

Chapter 5

"Is she loony-toons?" Fiona said to Madison at lunch.

They were standing on line in front of the hot food counter.

"Do you honestly think she can win?" Madison asked aloud. "Do you think Aimee even has a chance?"

"Baked beans, cheezy macaroni, or smashed potatoes?" the cafeteria server asked. Her stained name tag read GILDA Z and she liked to crack jokes as she ladled out the food.

"Macaroni, please," Madison said politely.

"Good for your noodle." Gilda laughed, scooping out the pasta. "Now, skedoodle!"

"She freaks me out," Fiona whispered.

"Hey, you guys." Aimee arrived, breathless. She twirled up to her friends like the perfect ballerina

she was and slid in behind Madison and Fiona with an empty tray.

"No cutting," a kid yelled.

Aimee snapped back, "They were saving my place."

"Where were you?" Fiona asked.

"Class." Aimee's eyes scanned the tub of neon-yellow-colored macaroni. "Hey, Maddie, did you know that that tub of food has more fat in it than—"

"Aim! I'm eating that," Madison yelled. "Shhhh!"

Gilda Z. slopped vegetables onto Aimee's tray.

On the way to the orange table at the back of the room (their *regular* lunch table), Madison, Fiona, and Aimee passed Ivy and her drones, Rose and Joan. The enemy was seated at their usual yellow table, chatting away.

"Hey, Finnster!" Hart Jones called out from nearby.

Madison groaned under her breath but didn't say hello.

"Why does he call you that?" Fiona asked.

Madison shook her head, and sat down to eat her lunch. Sitting there, looking out across the student body, Madison felt herself shrinking—and over-thinking.

Why did Hart keep calling her Finnster?

How could she figure out a way to help Aimee win, help Ivy get beaten, and still work on the Web site fairly?

How did she get herself into this mess?

With each bite of cheezy macaroni, Madison was feeling more and more conflicted about her role in the upcoming election.

"Maddie, did you hear what I said?" Fiona slurped her milk.

"Wha?" Madison was acting more spaced-out than Fiona. Apparently, her friends had been trying to get her attention for a minute or so.

"I was just telling Aimee that I really think she can win," Fiona said. "If we help."

"I guess so."

Aimee made a face. "Hey, you're supposed to be on my side! Whaddya mean, 'I guess'?"

Madison snapped back to attention. "Sorry. I was just thinking."

"Oh! I almost forgot," Fiona said. "The coaches told us they would put the soccer lists up today. We can find out if we made the JV team, Madison." She slid out from behind the orange table.

"I can't believe Fiona got you to try out for a sport, Maddie."

Last weekend, Madison had joined Fiona at soccer tryouts. Fiona had been on four different soccer teams back in California before she moved to Far Hills. Everyone who tried out was blown away by Fiona's running and passing and overall soccer skills.

"Of course *you* made it. You were born wearing soccer cleats, right?" Madison dragged her fork

across her plate. "Fiona, you'd better give up on me. I just don't have a chance at getting on."

"It would be fun to do it together, though." Fiona was still hopeful. "Maybe you can get picked as an alternate."

"Well, you check the list. I'm too scared to look," Madison said.

"Okay, then." Fiona was standing up, slinging her bag over her shoulder. "But you should think positive."

"I am positive," Madison said, "positively sure I didn't make it."

"Well, if I don't see you after school, I'll IM you later, 'kay?" Fiona said. "'Bye, Aimee."

Madison knew she hadn't made the team because during tryouts, she'd passed the ball to the wrong person *twice* coming down the field and she had touched the ball with her hand like four times. That was a no-no.

But deep down, she didn't mind. The whole reason for trying out wasn't so Madison could become the next soccer star. It was just a way to get closer and have something else in common with Fiona. With soccer practices happening practically every afternoon, Madison wouldn't be seeing very much of Fiona during the fall, especially not on weekends with out-of-town games.

"Don't worry about soccer, Maddie," Aimee said, trying to make her friend feel better.

Madison picked pieces of coconut off the cake on her tray. She said nothing.

"Hey, did you see what Ivy was wearing today?" Aimee said. "She thinks she is so *all that*. Please."

Madison glanced over at Poison and her drones. Ivy had on a tight pink T-shirt that said FAR OUT and a long camouflage-patterned cargo skirt. Madison recognized it from the pages of her favorite online catalog. She hated the way Ivy looked good wearing anything. It wasn't fair.

Just as she was looking that direction, Madison also saw Ivy motion to Hart Jones to come over to her table. Chet and Hart sat down there together for a moment or two.

"Don't look now," Aimee leaned into Madison, "but there's a teacher headed right this—"

"There you are!" Mrs. Wing rushed up to Madison's table carrying a clipboard and a cup of coffee that looked like it was about to spill. "Oh! I have been looking for you all over. We need to talk about the election site. Mr. Bernard is so pleased that you will be helping out. Can you come by my classroom after school?"

Madison shrugged. "Okay."

"Of course!" Mrs. Wing said. "Now, I should tell you that I have two other students helping out, too. Andrew Maxwell and Walter Diaz."

"Drew?" Madison wasn't sure she'd heard Mrs. Wing correctly. "Walter?"

"They'll be working with me on data entry. You know, candidate profiles and that stuff. They volunteered to help. Said they just really had to be involved in some way. Isn't that nice?"

Aimee stood up. "Look, I gotta go, Maddie. Sorry to interrupt, Mrs. Wing." She disappeared before Madison had time to respond.

"Well, then, I'll see you and Drew and Walter after classes then," Mrs. Wing said. Then she disappeared, too, out the door going in the direction of the teachers' lounge.

Madison looked up to see that three-quarters of the 12:00 cafeteria group had left. Madison stood up. No one sat in the lunchroom *alone*! She dumped her uneaten food.

"Hey, Maddie!" Drew caught up with Madison in the hallway on his way to social studies class.

"Hey," Madison said. "So I wanted to ask you—"

"What?" Drew asked.

"Okay." Madison bit her lip. "I wanted to ask you. . . . Since when are you and Egg signed up to help with Mrs. Wing's thing?"

He stammered. "H-h-help? Well, I don't know. We just figured it was a cool thing to do. After yesterday, we got to talking. That's all. We wanted to be a part of the Web site."

Drew usually got to be a part of whatever he wanted. His father was a richer-than-rich inventor who always gave his son the newest, coolest gadgets.

Once Drew had an actual spy pen with a teeny-weeny camera inside it, as if someone had slipped James Bond's toy into his pocket.

Madison made a face. "Did Egg put you up to this?"

"Egg?" Drew acted surprised. "Like I said, we thought about it together."

"Yeah, but it's really him," Madison mumbled. "He's so competitive."

"Maybe a little," Drew said. "But he's also smart. Don't you think it will be fun if we all do it together?"

"I guess," Madison sighed. She wasn't totally convinced.

After school, by the time the three of them met up together in room 510 to start the Web site project, Madison was getting used to the idea of Egg and Drew helping. She had to admit that the boys were as good as she was (if not better) with computer stuff. Especially Drew. Even though Egg was a bigmouth about his skills, Madison knew for a fact that Drew had a much higher score at Age of Empires than Egg. He was just a lot quieter about what he knew and didn't know.

Mrs. Wing walked into the technology lab, arms filled with folders and envelopes. "Walter, could you help me here?"

While Egg rescued the folders from Mrs. Wing's arms, Madison and Drew logged onto their computer

stations. They went to the text prompts first. There was information to be input on the site. It was the information Madison had retrieved from the newspaper room.

"I'll be right back," Mrs. Wing said. "I need to run back to the office. Start inputting this information and I'll be back shortly."

"Did you read this?" Drew was typing in Ivy's profile and statement of purpose. "She says, 'I promise that when I am elected, I will make this the best junior high in the world.' Is she kidding? In the *world*? Talk about making stuff up. She doesn't even say *how* she's going to do it."

Egg looked at her photo. "Yeah, but she's still a hottie."

"Egg!" Madison groaned. No matter how evil Ivy acted, all Egg really seemed to notice was how she *looked*.

"She comes off like a total robot," Drew said.

"Aimee isn't a robot," Madison said. "Read something from her profile."

Drew shuffled the pages. "'I, Aimee Gillespie, promise that when I am elected, I will make this the best junior high in the world.'"

Egg cackled. "Hah! She says the exact same thing as Poison Ivy!"

"Maybe we should change that," Drew said. "You have to fix what Aimee says."

"That wouldn't be fair," Egg said.

"Yeah, but Aimee is a way cooler candidate," Drew insisted.

Madison just listened as the boys bickered back and forth. She was busy scrolling through the pages of programming code to make sure the information had all been input correctly.

"Do you like Aimee or something?" Egg asked.

"Aimee?" Drew replied. "I like her. She's nice. She's a good dancer."

Madison jumped into the conversation. "No, he means *like* her, like her."

"Yeah, Drew, do you like her, *like* her?"

"What?" Drew was taken aback. "Well, not exactly," he gulped. "I mean, not in the *like* like kind of way." He was very surprised by this new line of questioning. "No way, Jose. I don't like Aimee. No."

"Who do you like?" Egg prodded him.

"Yeah," Madison chimed in. "Who?"

Drew shook off the question. "We should input this before Mrs. Wing comes back."

At first Madison had wanted this election project all for herself, but she felt different as time passed. Maybe it wasn't so weird with the three of them working on the site. Madison had always assumed Egg and his pals were abnormal. But Drew and Egg could set up the Web pages faster than fast.

Madison remembered that Drew was a cousin of Hart Jones's. Maybe she could ask him questions about who Hart liked, too?

"Hey, Drew, what's the deal with your cousin Hart?"

"Hart? What does Hart have to do with anything?" Drew looked confused.

"Oh, I was just wondering—"

"Hart's a fart," Egg interrupted. Drew snorted. Madison just rolled her eyes. Sometimes boys could really be so immature. She'd save her questions for another time.

"Just forget it," Madison said.

She was glad to drop the subject. Madison had no logical reason whatsoever to be asking about Hart. She didn't want Egg or Drew to get the wrong idea about her interest. She didn't want them to get *any* idea.

When she got home to Aimee's, Madison found her e-mailbox icon blinking.

Seeing that she had mail lifted her spirits.

From: ff_BudgeFilms
To: MadFinn
Subject: Phone Call
Date: Tues 12 Sept 1:21 PM

Hello, sweetie. I tried to call you before sleep tonite (we're 6 hours ahead, remember?) but the line was busy for an hour! Aimee's brothers are always on that phone, I'm sure. Well, I just wanted to say that I miss you very much. Are you okay at

school? I'm sorry to be gone for so long. I promise, no more long trips.

Did I mention that it is very rainy here?

Je t'aime, ma cherie.

Reading the mail left Madison disappointed. She wanted to hear Mom's voice for real. She wanted someone to tell her that the election would turn out okay. But this would have to do. Calling France was way too expensive, Madison told herself, especially from someone else's house.

A new note from Bigwheels popped up after Mom's. Madison had hit the e-mail jackpot.

From: Bigwheels
To: MadFinn
Subject: Re: School elections and stuff
Date: Tues 12 Sept 5:01 PM

Yes, I think boys are all weird. No, I do not have a boyfriend. (I used to have a pen pal in Spain named Robbie, but he moved and I never got his new address. I met him through my parents. My Dad had a client who lived there. Robbie

was so nice but he made me a little nervous and in general I think boys make me nervous.)

I never feel like myself when I am with boys. Do you? I do have crushes on movie stars sometimes though. Do you?

Do you like a person at your school? Is that why you feel weird? I am sure whoever you like will like you right back if you are just honest with him. I may not be the best person to ask for advice, but I definitely think you need to be honest. Honesty is the best policy. Just don't be nervous if you can help it.

I actually meant to tell you that I was just elected last week as class rep in my class, so I know EXACTLY what you mean by annoying elections. Good luck with yours! Why aren't u running for class prez? You sound so smart.

I have a question for you: do you have brothers and sisters? I have one sister and one brother who are

both younger than me. My brother is only four. He is a pest.

Yours till the moon beams,

Bigwheels

p.s. If your mom is away, y don't u call ur Dad? My dad always makes me feel much better. Yesterday my daddy got me flowers.

Madison's Dad got her flowers sometimes, too. But today, when Madison dialed his cell phone, she only got Dad's recording.

Please—leave—message. Beeeeeeep.

"Uh, Dad . . . this is Maddie and . . . I am calling because I need . . . well, I miss . . . when you get this please call me back I don't know when . . . I just wanted to say hi and good-bye so . . . hi . . . and good-bye. Okay, that's all. Don't forget I'm at Aimee's house."

No sooner had Madison rested the phone back into its cradle, when Mr. Gillespie screeched from downstairs.

"Soup's on!"

So far they were having dinner every night at six o'clock on the dot. Tonight there was baked whole-wheat bread (all-natural and organic, of course), grilled vegetables, and some other macrobiotic food.

Madison wasn't too sure what half of the food on her plate was. She was now eating the exact *opposite* of Mom's Scary Dinners.

Aimee's other two brothers, Dean and Doug, were the only ones at the table tonight and they didn't talk much. It wasn't the same as the previous night's burps and urps. Mayhem tonight was minimal.

Dean was a senior in high school who worried and talked more about his Camry and hot girls than anything else. Doug was a ninth grader who Madison sometimes saw at school but who never said much of anything, let alone "Hiya, Madison." He didn't seem to care about anything more than his high-tech calculator and baseball. Tonight Doug and Dean were arguing about catchers. Madison tuned right out.

Blossom brushed Madison's foot and she sneaked a grilled piece of zucchini under the table. A second later Blossom woofed it up. Even the dog liked vegetables in this house.

"Mmhey, Mmmaddie." Aimee chewed with her mouth full sometimes. "Mmmell my dad—"

"Pass the pepper, please," Mr. Gillespie said.

"Mmhow mmis the mmelection mmmweb site?"

Madison looked at Aimee for a moment like she had three heads, and then finally figured out how to translate her mouth-full-of-food lingo: *How is the election site?*

"Fine," Madison answered, picking at the couscous on her plate. It was brown bulgur wheat, Mrs. Gillespie had said, but it looked more like coarse sand. *Sand?* She would have given anything in that moment for a cheeseburger. Why would anyone want to eat sand?

It always grossed out Madison that Aimee loved brussels sprouts more than burgers. Aimee liked eggplant, okra, and lima beans, too! She was already on her second helping of sand.

"Madison," Mrs. Gillespie said, "have you heard from your mom?"

"Yes, she wrote me an e-mail." Madison shrugged. "I miss her. I mean, I *missed* her. She tried to call and the line was busy."

"Well, I bet she'll call again either late tonight or tomorrow, depending on her schedule." Mrs. Gillespie's radar was up. She could tell Madison was homesick. "I'm sure your mom is having a great old time over there. I am so envious of her traveling around the world. That must be so—"

"Pass the salt, please," Mr. Gillespie interrupted.

"Mmddad!" Aimee groaned, giving her Dad an evil look.

Mrs. Gillespie kept right on talking, about how smart Madison's mom was, and independent, and adventurous. . . .

And never home, Madison thought. By now, Blossom and Phin were begging under the table. She

shoved another grilled pepper downward. There was a collection of all-natural food scraps under the table.

It seemed that feeding dinner to the dog was only increasing *Madison*'s appetite. Madison realized she would have to ask Aimee for a peanut-butter sandwich after dinner. Her stomach grumbled and she prayed no one else had heard it.

"You know, Mrs. Gillespie," Madison said as they helped clear the sand and sprouts off the table. "I really appreciate your having me stay here. And Phinnie, too."

Mrs. Gillespie ran her hand over Madison's shoulder and squeezed. "I know. Maddie, you're like family here. You and Aimee have been friends since you were *born*."

Phinnie growled, "Rowrroooo!" It was like he knew what people were saying. Or at least knew when people were talking about him.

Aimee picked a sponge fight in the kitchen, and the two pals were throwing wet dishrags around, putting on fake accents, when Mrs. Gillespie called Maddie back into the dining room.

"Oh my gosh!" she cried, as she walked in.

Too late.

Mrs. Gillespie was down on her hands and knees picking up the mess.

"Oh, Mrs. Gillsepie, I am so sorry, I am—"

Aimee's mother just grinned. "Next time, you tell

me what you want, okay? No more secret dumping on the carpet. I don't think Phin or Blossom is much of a vegetarian. And neither are you."

"I like vegetables," Madison stammered. "It's just that—"

She didn't know what else to say. She could feel her feet telling her to run away, as always. But of course she didn't go anywhere. She kneeled down and picked up a soggy carrot. Phin had half-chewed it and dragged it across the floor.

"Maddie," Mrs. Gillespie said again, "you don't have to pretend around here. So you can talk to me if you want. You can tell me things . . . I meant what I said before. I think of you like my second daughter, okay?"

Mrs. Gillespie always knew how to say just the right thing. It really *was* like having a substitute mom when Mom was out of town. Madison couldn't decide if that was weird or if she was lucky or both.

When Aimee and Madison had finished up their social studies homework (from the one and only class they *did* have together), they sneaked out Aimee's bedroom window onto the roof. This was their secret place. It was the flat part of the roof, more like a patio where you could lay on your back and watch the stars. Aimee's dad had built a little lip around the roof to keep people away from the edge and close to the window.

"Gee, it smells like rain tonight, doesn't it?"

Aimee said as they lay back on the shingles.

Madison lay back again and searched the sky for the moon. Even with some stars, it was so dark out tonight that looking for a crescent moon was like searching for a fingernail paring in the sky.

"So, Maddie, tell me about the Web site," Aimee said.

Madison explained how she downloaded photos and information and Mrs. Wing helped them to code the information in a special way. Aimee was the biggest chatterbox, but she could also be a great listener.

"Oh, is that what happened to those election pictures I gave in when I announced I would run?"

Madison told her those had been uploaded, too. "Oh, did I tell you that Egg and Drew are part of the team now, too?" Madison added.

"Drew *Maxwell*?"

"Yeah." Madison nodded. "Mrs. Wing said they asked to be a part of it. They volunteered. Weird, huh?"

"Oh, really?" Aimee said. Madison detected a funny tone to her voice. "Do you think Drew did that to make sure I win or something?"

"What?"

"I'm just joking. Of course I know he's probably only doing it so he can—" Aimee cut herself short. "Well, I'm sure that's nice for you, having Egg and Drew around."

"It's okay."

Aimee pointed up into the sky. "Hey, is that yellow thing a planet or a UFO?"

"UFO. Totally! Aim, remember that alien dream you used to have as a kid?"

Aimee covered her eyes. "Why did you have to remind me? Now I'll never sleep tonight. Alien abductions. Spaceships. Weird machines. That gives me the jeebies."

Suddenly, a shooting star zipped past.

"Did you see that?" they said at the exact same time.

Then they laughed and made a wish with their eyes shut.

Madison felt serious all of a sudden and so she said, "Aimee, I want to make sure you know that I want you to win this election. I really, really want you to beat Ivy. I just wanted you to know that. I'm on your side."

"I know that, silly!" Aimee laughed. "I want to win, too. Not that I have any idea about how to be class president. Well, I have an idea about what I *could* be like. I guess I just did this because someone had to show Ivy she can't always have it *her* way."

"Too bad there isn't a talent contest as a part of elections. You could dance and win all the votes just like that."

"Just like *THAT*!" Aimee snapped her fingers.

"I think it's between you and Ivy, for real. Are you nervous?"

"*SO* nervous," Aimee said, hugging her knees.

The two stayed huddled under the chilly, speckled night sky for a while longer, enjoying their "slumber party." It was one of those moments you gulp and swallow to keep in your belly, in your heart, for always.

Then the phone rang.

"Hey, maybe it's your mom calling from France," Aimee yelped encouragingly, lunging back inside through the window to answer it.

Madison's stomach flip-flopped at the idea—but of course it wasn't Mom.

It was one of Aimee's brother's girlfriends.

"Dean has like ten different girlfriends," Aimee said. "He's so hideous. Who would date him? Someone else hideous, I guess."

Madison giggled. "Doug's still a hottie!"

Aimee lightly punched Madison's shoulder. "Get *OUT*! Quit looking at my brothers! That's like . . . you shouldn't even joke about that kind of stuff." She was half-yelling and half-laughing. "Oh my *GOD*, can you imagine?"

Madison teased, "Maybe I'll marry one of them, Aimee, and we could be sisters for real. What do you think?"

Aimee made a face like she would throw up. "I think I'd rather be friends."

As they turned off the light to sleep, Madison imagined a day when she would be the one getting

a late-night call from a boyfriend. Maybe boys weren't so terrible.

"Aimee?" Madison whispered after a few minutes in the darkness.

There was no answer.

"Aimee, are you there?" Madison asked again. She wanted to talk about boys and parents and family and the Far Hills elections for just a little bit longer.

But Aimee was already fast asleep.

Madison wished talking in your sleep meant having *real* conversations with each other. That way she and Aimee could keep on talking until the sun came up again.

She reached over the edge of the bed and placed her hand on Phin's back. His side heaved with little, fast breaths, like the kind you have when you're in the middle of a doggy dream.

Chapter 6

Dad

Dad called this morning. He and I are ON for dinner tonight and I cannot wait. I can't wait for so many reasons. First, because I want to see my dad of course. Then, because I want to eat meat or something that isn't sand. And also because I just want to be somewhere that really is my family. Even though the Gillespies are the best and they take good care of me it's not the same.

I told Dad all about the election Web site and stuff. He sounded really excited, so we'll probably spend all of our reunion dinner talking about that. I like these

dinners because it's our special time just him and me. Oh, and Dad says he has a big surprise for me. I love surprises.

At 6:28 on the dot, Dad pulled into the Gillespies' driveway.

Dad had said he would show up at Aimee's at six o'clock to pick Madison up. Madison knew that really meant he'd be there at 6:30, of course, but she didn't mind. He was always late.

Madison smoothed out her peasant skirt (she had borrowed it from Aimee, and it was a little snug, but so pretty), checked her hair in the mirror (she wore it down tonight with her sapphire-blue barrettes), adjusted her favorite moonstone earrings (the same ones Dad gave to her when school first started), and smelled her armpits, of course. She always did that just to make sure she wasn't sweating too much. It was a gross thing to do, but it was *way* less gross than being a stink bomb in the middle of dinner. Luckily, even though it was humid tonight, Madison smelled like Lovely Ylang-Ylang. She'd borrowed some of Aimee's all-natural perfume.

"'Bye," Aimee yelled out as Madison walked down the porch steps. "You look great! Nice skirt."

"Ha ha!" Madison joked back. But she really did feel great.

For the first time in a few days, she felt like she was finally going to get some of her own family TLC. She needed some of that.

Dad was always so sweet, and she needed sweet. And he said that he had a surprise. Maybe he had another present? Madison couldn't believe she'd expect that, but the thought whizzed through her mind. The only benefit to Mom and Dad being away a lot was the fact that they sometimes got her cool stuff. As soon as she thought that, Madison felt guilty. What was she doing thinking about "stuff"? She told herself that she shouldn't—

Stop over-thinking, a voice echoed in her head. Voice of Dad, of course.

"Well, don't you look lovely," Dad said in person a moment later. He opened his arms to give Maddie a great big squeeze as she approached his car. It was really dark because the side lawn light was broken, but Dad still noticed what she was wearing. He *always* noticed.

"Isn't that a nice skirt," he said. "Mmm, you smell lovely, too."

"Lovely Ylang-Ylang, actually." Madison smiled.

"What?" He laughed. "Wang wang?"

"Eelang-eelang, Daddy! Like the letter L."

"Oh."

From inside the front seat of the car a strange voice said, "Ylang-ylang is an essential oil, Jeffrey."

Madison stopped in her tracks. Her stomach did a *GIANT* flip-flop.

"Uh, hello? Do I know you?"

"No, but I have heard so much about you." A

woman opened the door and stepped into the half-light in the driveway.

Madison turned to her dad and then turned to the woman.

"I haven't heard *anything* about you." Madison looked right at her father. "Daddy?"

"Madison, meet Stephanie," he said suddenly, clapping his hands together. "She's going to be joining us for dinner. Isn't that great?"

"Great? Um . . . Daddy?"

The woman stuck out her hand. "I'm Stephanie Wolfe," she said. "I'm a friend of your father. It's so nice to meet you. As I said, I've heard—"

"What's nice about it? I didn't know you were coming." Madison abruptly opened the back door, slid inside, and pulled it shut.

From where she was sitting inside the car she could just make out the figures of Dad and Stephanie talking in the shadows. She couldn't hear what they were saying, but they were talking very fast.

Madison smoothed out her skirt again. It was hot inside that car. Her legs itched. Madison smelled her armpits again just in case. Nothing but ylang-ylang.

How could Dad have forgotten to tell her he was bringing someone to dinner . . . to their special *reunion* dinner? How could Dad be with another woman besides Mom? Was this his idea of a surprise?

Madison *hated* surprises.

Stephanie got into the front seat again. Madison could smell her hair spray. Madison hadn't been shoved into the backseat of this car since she and Mom and Dad took Phin to the vet more than a year ago. She always rode shotgun. *Always.*

A droplet of sweat ran down the back of Madison's neck.

"So your dad tells me that you're a real computer whiz, is that true?" Stephanie said in the half-darkness, turning her head to catch Madison's eye.

Madison avoided all eye contact.

Stephanie paused. "Look, Maddie, I know you're surprised by my being here. And I don't feel all that comfortable either, Maddie, to tell you the truth—"

"Steph!" Dad said, a little surprised.

"But, Maddie, let's try to make the best of it? I could leave if that would—"

"Then leave," Madison cut her off. "Leave. And stop calling me Maddie. No one calls me Maddie except people who are my friends. I don't even know you."

"Now, wait just a minute!" Dad yelled. "Do you have any manners, young lady? I want you to apolo—"

"Jeff, look out!"

Dad swerved to miss hitting a cat in the middle of the road.

"Stupid animal!" Dad barked.

Madison spoke up from the backseat. "Animals are NOT stupid."

Dad sighed, exasperated. Even from where she was crouched into the backseat, Madison could see Stephanie put her hand on Dad's knee. She just wanted to turn around and go right back to the Gillespies.

No sooner had they parked the car than Madison jumped ten paces ahead, rushing across the parking lot, taking two steps at a time up to the restaurant lobby, praying that Le Poisson would be air-conditioned. Of course it was nice and cold inside. Nice and *ice* cold.

Be careful what you wish for, Madison mused, shivering.

The maitre d' sat the threesome at a table near a giant fish tank. Madison was grateful. Fish could focus her *away* from Stephanie. She named a yellow-finned one Phin 2 in her mind and watched him swim behind a fake treasure chest to hide out. Madison wished she could hide out. It was like being in the real-life bigfishbowl.com.

When the waiter came to take their drink order, Madison asked for root beer, her favorite drink on the planet.

"No root beere," he said. "This eez French restau-rahn."

"No root beer? Then I'd like . . . a cream soda?"

"No creamy soda," he said, shaking his head.

"Ginger ale?" He nodded. *Finally.*

"One, please."

The waiter smiled as Stephanie ordered a wine spritzer on the rocks and Dad got his usual seltzer with lime.

All the Frenchy French waiters and the French words on the menu reminded Madison of one thing.

"You know, my Mom's in France," Madison said, staring right at Stephanie. "She's a really, really important film producer and she's making a documentary there. Right now she's scouting locations."

"Oh, really?" Stephanie pretended to be nice. "That sounds interesting."

"She's really, really important. Did I mention that?"

"Yes, you did. You did mention that," Stephanie said. For the first time, Madison noticed that Stephanie was actually kind of pretty. How annoying. Madison searched Stephanie's face for moles and wrinkles.

"Maddie," Dad started to say when it seemed like things had calmed down a little bit, "I really am sorry that I didn't tell you first about—"

"Whatever, Dad. No biggie, right?" Madison shrugged.

Dad was fumbling to speak, but Madison wouldn't even let him finish a sentence. She told them both about the election Web site start-up, Mrs.

Wing, and how Aimee was running for class president.

Stephanie acted interested. "Is that glitter nail polish you're wearing?" she asked Madison.

Madison frowned. "Yeah, but I ate most of it off." She saw that Stephanie had perfectly manicured pink nails.

"This dinner is turning out just great," Dad said. "And here I thought—" He laughed and grabbed a sesame roll out of the bread basket on the table, mumbling to himself a little.

That's when Madison caught Stephanie putting her hand on Dad's knee again. At least that's what it seemed like. They were sitting very close. *Too close.*

But Madison knew what to do.

When dinner was served, Madison watched and waited until Stephanie was ready to take the first big bite of her fish dinner.

That's when Madison said, "Um, Dad, did I tell you about Phin?"

Dad was laughing nervously at everything by now. "No, honey bear, what about him?"

"Well." Madison stared right at Stephanie as she started the story. "It's just that Phin has that stomach thing again, you know the bad sick thing where he can't stop pooping."

Stephanie made a disgusted face.

"Maddie!" Dad said, but Madison kept right on talking.

"Yeah, it's really gross. It was all over the carpet this morning and he just makes this awful noise when he's doing it and it smells and—"

"Madison!" Dad said again, a little louder.

Stephanie gulped and put down her fork.

"Oh!" Madison covered her mouth. "I'm sorry, Stephanie, were you eating?"

As Stephanie took a sip of water, Madison took a huge bite of her own dinner. Her "Le Poisson" hamburger was well done, just the way she liked it.

 Dad

There are not enough words in the entire Webster's Dictionary to explain what I am feeling right now but I would have to say that CRUSHED is it. I came home right after dinner and I feel disgusting. How could Dad have done that to me? I was so freaked out during dinner I ordered eight ginger ales and drank every single one! I had to pee the whole time. And I don't even like ginger ale. How could we go to a restaurant that doesn't serve root beer?

Now I really wish Mom were home. I wish I could call France. I wish I had a brother or sister to share this with. Aimee is downstairs right now watching the end of some movie with Roger and I just can't go in the TV room all sad and depressed and make this scene and call attention to

myself. I just can't. I hate Daddy for this. No, I hate Stephanie more. Now I hate this feeling of hating people!

Madison closed the file, plugged her modem line into the phone jack, and dialed up the Internet.

She needed to chat—NOW.

In the bigfishbowl.com main lobby, or "fish tank" area, Madison searched the room lists and eavesdropped on a few rooms. Where was Bigwheels? She needed Bigwheels in a big way—NOW.

SHARK (Moderator)
GottaWIN
2good2be2
TellMeAStORY
Iluvrich
Intoredgiant
Screammeem
JimD71068
URPrincess
NvrSAYNvr
Pokemenow
654aqua

<Screammeem>: 12345
MadFinn has entered the room.
<URPrincess>: NO!!!!!
<Screammeem>: Anyone from WV?
<NvrSAYNvr>: Hey MadFinn A/S/L?
<Screammeem>: Anyone from WV HELLO

<Iluvrich>: How r u?
<654aqua>: heymeem, GAL
<Screammeem>: Wuzup with skool/>?
It's kool
Intoredgiant has left the room.
gonefishin has entered the room.
<URPrincess>: LMSO School is SO NOT
:~/
<MadFinn>: :—0
<MadFinn>: What is 12345?
<NvrSAYNvr>: Hey gonefishin A/S/L?
<Screammeem>: anyone play soccer?
<Gonefishin>: 13/M/NY
URPrincess has left the room.
<TellMeaStoRY>:Have u seen Tidal
Wave the movie?
<NvrSAYNvr>: anyone wanna private
chat
<TellMeaStoRY>: it is soooooo good
and so scary
<Screammeem>: am in soccr leage
doggydave has entered the room.
<gonefishin>: ^5 meem! How r u?
<screammeem>: IM Me
<gonefishin>: c ya sucka
<SHARK>: Watch your language, please
<MadFinn>: *poof*

Bigwheels must have been asleep or something even though it was only dinnertime where she was.

Maybe she was doing her homework?

She definitely wasn't in this chat room. She wasn't even online.

Madison checked her e-mail just in case.

```
Mailbox Empty
```

As soon as she saw the word "empty," the heaviness in her ribs pushed up into her throat. It was like nausea, only she knew she wasn't sick. Madison shut down the computer, shut off the light, and buried her face into one of Aimee's pillows. She hated crying in a strange place.

After ten seconds, her nose was running and she was drooling, too. Madison always drooled when she cried. Phinnie heard her and jumped onto the bed too. He was licking the salty tears off her face and wiggling his curlicue tail.

Dogs always can tell when people are really sad. Madison was glad that Phinnie was around. Blossom was at the bottom of the bed the whole time, jumping, but basset hounds aren't so good at getting onto high places.

"Maddie?" The light clicked on all of a sudden and Aimee rushed over to the bed. "Maddie, I heard you . . . what happened? Are you okay?"

Madison sniffled but no words would come out. She tried to catch her breath in between hiccups and tears. She was crying hard by now.

"Aimee?" Mrs. Gillespie walked into the room

next. "Is everything all right in here? I heard—"

Aimee shrugged. "Maddie's all bummed out. Her Dad brought a date to dinner and she didn't know about it and—"

"I—was—so—up—set—"

Madison coughed each syllable and Aimee's mother sat down on the edge of the bed and rubbed her back. "Take a deep breath, Maddie. You'll be okay, dear. I know it's got to be hard. All this change."

Madison gasped and sniffled and choked on her own words.

"Change—Steph—stink—Dad—"

She wasn't making any sense.

Mrs. Gillespie ran a cool hand across Madison's neck to get her to stop crying. Her hands were as soft as the satin edge of a blanket. "Maddie," she asked, "Should we call your mom?"

Madison wiped her eyes and blinked. "In Paris?"

"I think we should." Mrs. Gillespie pulled a few strands of hair out of Maddie's wet eyes. "I know your mom would want to be right here, right now, giving you a hug and telling you everything is okay. You should call her."

Madison sniffled. "You mean it?"

"Yes, let's call her. Right now."

Madison's could feel her heartbeat quicken at the prospect of hearing Mom's voice. Together, Mrs. Gillespie, Aimee, and Madison dialed the international

operator and called Mom all the way over in France. It was 5:30 in the morning, but Madison didn't care about waking Mom up.

Madison Finn was caught between a dad and a date and all she needed was to know that her Mom was there, somewhere. She needed to know she wasn't crazy for feeling all knotted up inside. That everything with Dad and Ivy and school and elections would all work out. That feeling like a baby was an okay way to feel right now.

Sometimes only a mom can tell you things so you believe them.

Chapter 7

From: MadFinn
To: ff_BudgeFilms
PRIORITY MAIL
Subject: Last Night
Date: Thurs 14 Sept 7:19 AM

Mom I am so sorry I woke you up. But I slept so well after we got off the phone. I didn't realize I missed you so much. Is that weird? I mean, last night I was just so sad. And it wasn't Dad's fault. I don't want to make it sound like he's bad, because I know you think that sometimes. No, it was just everything happening all at the same time.

Phinnie slept under the blankets with me for a little while, too, just like you said. Until he got hot and started snoring like he does. Oh well. Now Aimee's bed smells like dog.

Thanks again Mom. I am really sorry again for getting you up to the phone at like 4 your time or whenever it was. I know you are busy and that the movie is important too.

By the way, Dad called this morning first thing to check on me. He says no more surprise dinners so that's a good thing, right?
Please come home soon.
Love, me :>)

After all the excitement of yesterday, Madison made like a zombie and zoned out through her morning classes. She didn't come out of her trance until noon, when she, Drew, Egg, and Mrs. Wing spent lunch period huddled over a computer monitor inside the tech lab, checking out the day's progress on the Far Hills site. Despite her anxiety from yesterday, it felt good to Madison to be working on the election Web pages again with the boys. Plus, serious computer

work got Madison's mind off any and all "bad" subjects: last night's dinner with Dad and Stephanie; Hart calling her Finnster (four times so far that week); and Poison Ivy, of course.

The home page was looking good.

```
WELCOME TO FAR HILLS JUNIOR HIGH
1753 Far Hills Avenue
Far Hills, New York

School Principal: Mr. Joe Bernard
Assistant Principal: Mrs. Bonnie Goode
Web page designed and created by FH
Faculty and Students

Elections coordinator: Madison Finn
Data entry: Drew Maxwell
Online programs: Walter Diaz
Student adviser: Mrs. Isabel Wing

Note: Please adjust your screen to 640x480
full window for optimal
viewing.
```

The Web page layout was a basic model, devoted to helping direct students to the polling areas, but Madison knew it had big possibilities. She hoped that the school Web site could change the way *everything* was done and how everyone communicated at school. She had the entire Web site menu mapped out in her imagination.

Homepage
Schedules
Assignments & Calendars
Clubs & Organizations
Sports & Teams
The Far Hills Journal
Faculty
Links
The I Don't Like Ivy Daly at All Club

Sometimes she got a little carried away.

Faculty and students were logging on to the Web page on different computers all over school. Not just in the tech lab, but in the library media center, the administrative offices, the reading room, and even in the school newspaper headquarters.

After being up only two days, it was already a huge success. The word was out.

Madison and her friends felt so proud.

Thanks to Mrs. Wing, all of this was happening. Madison noticed how Mrs. Wing's iridescent shell earrings shimmered like magic each time they caught sunlight. They reminded Madison of the moonstone earrings Dad had bought her for seventh grade good luck. Working on computers was working magic on Maddie.

One of the most important tasks of Mrs. Wing's election Web site team was to get the online voting tabulation system to work properly. A Far Hills ninth-grade math teacher named Mr. Lynch installed more

memory in all computers to make the election program work faster. He stayed around to help supervise the HTML coding, the special Web site-making language. Neither Madison nor the others knew HTML very well. Madison realized that even a smarter-than-smart teacher like Mrs. Wing needed help sometimes. Things really happened when they all worked together.

They didn't have a lot of time to do it. Mrs. Wing was pulling out all the stops. Next week was the election assembly and they had to be ready.

Drew and Egg worked together during their free period to get the student polls in order. The first poll results were already in.

```
What school issue is important to
you in this year's election? Please
check off your #1 choice.

1. Homework 51%
2. Cafeteria food 16%
3. After-school activities 14%
4. Sports 10%
5. Computer science 7%
6. Other 2%
```

One by one, the three of them checked through other grades' Web pages for the status of all the candidates for the offices of president, vice president, class treasurer, secretary, and class reps.

Everything looked fine, especially the seventh grade pages.

Drew brought up the Montrell Morris candidate page. Montrell had written a poem for his page that ended with the lines: "How do you spell Montrell? W-I-N-N-E-R."

Then Drew glanced over the Tommy Kwong page. Tommy just had one banner across the top: "TOTALLY TOMMY." Both Tommy's and Montrell's photos were a little blurry, but the links on their pages all worked.

Egg opened up to the page marked Ivy Daly. Everything looked in order there, too, especially Ivy's perfect red hair. He had to comment on that.

"You can't tell me this girl is not hot," Egg said.

Madison just rolled her eyes. She leaned over Egg's shoulder and clicked NEXT. It moved along to Aimee's page.

"Whoa!" Egg said with a start.

Madison stopped, blinked, and clicked the refresh button to reload the page.

"Wait! Hold up!" Egg squirmed around in the chair. "Did you see that?"

Madison punched at the keys frantically.

"What is THAT?" Drew added. He was now looking over Drew's other shoulder as the page reappeared. "Maddie, that is not Aimee."

Madison shook her head. She couldn't believe what she was seeing.

The image up on the screen next to "Aimee

Gillespie" was most definitely *not* Aimee. Not at all. On the computer screen, in the spot where Aimee's photograph had been, was a photograph of an ugly, spiny, old lizard.

"A heloderma!" Madison shrieked. "How did a helo—"

"Hello—*huh*?" Drew wrinkled his nose.

"A heloderma! A gila monster! A LIZARD!" said Madison.

"How do you know that?" Egg asked.

"Is this some kind of joke!" Madison squealed a little louder. "Did one of you guys do this?"

"Don't look at me!" Drew was *very* confused.

Egg shook his head. "Hey, I know I cause trouble, but this is like way beyond me."

"Then who put a gila monster up there? This is AWFUL!"

"Since when do you know gila monsters, Maddie? What, did you see one when you and your mom were in Brazil or something?" Egg blurted out.

Madison didn't like the way he was asking her questions. She pointed at the monitor. "Are you responsible for this, Egg Diaz? Is this how you get back at me?"

"Get back at you for what?" Egg said. "You know, Drew, I think Aimee and gila actually look a little the same. Whaddya say?"

Madison almost laughed—but she didn't.

"Put a lid on it, Egg," Drew said. He pinched Egg's arm.

Egg winced in pain. "Owwwch. What did you do that for?"

"Quick!" Madison tapped at the keyboard. "You guys, how many hits has the page received today?"

Egg read the number off the screen. "Two-hundred and ninety-one. Jeez, that's a lot of gila monster lovers."

"EGG! I'M SERIOUS!"

Mrs. Wing dashed back into the classroom at that exact moment and rushed over to help. She knew exactly how to fix the screen with all joking aside.

In only a few minutes the four of them were able to remove gila and get back Aimee.

Madison just kept shaking her head. "I don't understand. Yesterday we were here. We were here and everything seemed fine. . . . Aimee *looked* like Aimee, not like some—"

"Lizard?" Egg interjected. Madison shot him a look.

"Well, when was the last time you checked the site?" Mrs. Wing asked Madison. "This is a breach of the site. We need to look into it."

"Breach?" Madison let out a huge sigh. "I'm sorry, I'm sorry," she kept apologizing. She was crushed by the thought that somehow she'd failed. "This is all my fault. I must have done something—I'm sorry!"

"Madison, calm down. Now, we've deleted the photo of the—"

"Lizard," Egg piped up again. Madison shot him another look.

Drew gave him a noogie on the side of his arm.

"Stop!" Egg said.

"Would you two please relax?" Mrs. Wing said.

She made it clear that she would file a memo to administration, but that it was probably an "isolated incident," so no, they didn't have to cause a big fuss.

"However," Mrs. Wing added, "I think you three need to keep a closer watch on these pages just to make sure that we don't have any *more* funny stuff, okay? People like to play jokes, especially around election time. Be sure to let me know if anything else comes up, will you?"

Madison nodded emphatically, relieved that no more would be said about the lizard. She never wanted to see its spiny little body again, and she hoped that Aimee hadn't seen it—*ever.*

Unfortunately, by the end of the day, most of the teachers and students, and even Principal Bernard had seen it. Everyone *including* Aimee.

A wisecracking eighth grader had found the messed-up page and printed out a hard copy that got stuck up on the elevator bulletin board. Another kid posted a copy in the girl's bathroom with a note written in pencil: "LIZ" GILLESPIE FOR CLASS PREZ.

It was a disaster.

"Maddie, how could this have happened? I thought you were in charge of the election Web

site! I thought you were helping with my campaign! I thought you were MY FRIEND!" Aimee shrieked as she confronted Maddie in a deserted stairwell. Her voice ricocheted off the walls and windows.

"Aimee, pleasepleaseplease let me explain," Madison pleaded. "I am so so so so so sorry that it ever happened. But we fixed it. I mean we didn't do it on purpose. . . ."

"I don't think you understand how embarrassing this is," Aimee said, shaking a little. Usually she looked graceful, but now she was sputtering. "Look, you're responsible for the Web site, right?"

"I know, I know. I feel awful." At this point, Madison was tempted to get down on her knees. She didn't want Aimee to be mad or sad.

"Maddie, who would do this? Are you gonna find out who? Oh my GOD I am so embarrassed. I AM MORTIFIED."

Aimee didn't want *anything* to get in the way of her race to whup Ivy Daly in the school election. Madison knew a thing or two about awful embarrassing moments. She was often on the run from embarrassment.

"Can we please stop yelling?" Madison said softly. She saw imaginary steam steaming out of Aimee's ears, she looked *that* mad.

Suddenly, a fire door opened one flight up. Aimee and Madison clammed up. They waited to hear a second door creak open and slam shut.

"Wait!" Aimee shouted when the door slammed.

"What?" Madison was surprised.

"It wasn't you!" Aimee cried out, coming to a sudden realization. "Maddie, wait! I know who did this. This isn't *your* fault!"

"That's what I've been saying." Madison's eyes glazed over.

"And if it isn't your fault and it isn't Egg's fault and it isn't Drew's fault . . ."

"Then who?" Madison wondered aloud.

"This is Ivy Daly's fault! Of course! It has to be Poison Ivy! Think about it, Maddie. She probably did it because she was annoyed at me because my profile was better and she just *knew* I would win. So she logged on to the site, went online, and ruined my photo."

Madison thought for a minute.

"Doesn't that sound just like her?" Aimee said accusingly.

"Well . . ." Madison took a deep breath. "I dunno."

"Maddie!" Aimee insisted. "It has to be her! Who *else* would do this?"

Madison sighed again. She wanted Ivy to lose the school election as much as Aimee did, but she didn't want to accuse her of something like this—*did she*?

"Aimee, do you really think she would think of something like this? It seems a little shady, even for her."

"Absolutely. And now the joke is gonna be on Ivy. I'm gonna tell *everyone* at school tomorrow about what she did."

"Wait. I think we should find out for sure if she did it first," Madison said.

"Wait? Geesh, Maddie, whose side are you on?"

Madison was never on someone's "side." She was in the middle, as usual. "After all," she wanted to scream to Aimee, "accusing Ivy doesn't even make sense."

As the night wore on Aimee became more and more convinced that Ivy was the culprit. Madison silently grew more and more convinced that Ivy *wasn't* responsible. First, Ivy was so good at computers. Second, Ivy was the kind of meanie who said stuff to your face—not behind your back. Some other hacker had to have done it.

But *who*?

It was an election Web site mystery.

Chapter 8

Roger

Sometimes I wish I had an older brother like Roger Gillespie. Does Aimee know how great it is to have someone listen and *really* listen, not the kind of listening moms and dads do because they want to protect you and play it safe? Roger listens like he wants to really help.

This morning Aimee had to leave for her dance practice at like 6:30 and I was talking to Roger at breakfast about the problems we had with the election Web site. I asked him what I should do since Aimee was saying Ivy had put the lizard on the Web site but I didn't think so. I don't think Ivy even knows what a gila monster is.

Roger says don't put myself in the middle.

He says maybe being in the middle is why I feel crushed by different things, like being the meat in a sandwich or something.

Rude Awakening: I'm sandwich meat? No wonder boys don't like me.

After adding to some pages in her files, Madison ducked into her favorite online shopping site. It was a place where you could buy clothes and books and candles and other cool objects. She wrote down the online code and inventory numbers for a few things she desperately wanted. She knew when Mom came back home, the items would probably never get ordered, but she still liked to think about having them.

SWTTLK09214Q	Zipper Sweater with Flower Appliqué
SWTTLK09203Q	Cargo Pantskirt Camouflage Pattern
SWTTLK09239Q	Fuzzy Scrapbook
SWTTLK09218Q	Baby Tee (Orange Neon)

By the time Madison got into school that morning, her head was overflowing with over-thoughts about boys and clothes, and, of course, the election. She headed straight for Mrs. Wing's classroom.

"Madison!" Mrs. Wing cried out as soon as Madison walked into the room.

Egg was in the room, too. Drew wasn't in school yet.

"Madison, we have a problem," Egg said in an announcer's voice.

Madison's stomach flopped. She imagined Aimee's Web page again: *Attack of the Gila Monster, Part Two.* She was afraid to look.

"See?" Egg pointed to the computer screen. "Problem."

Madison's heart sank.

"What is this?" Mrs. Wing asked, pointing at Ivy's page.

There, under the flashing name IVY DALY was not a photo of a seventh grader with picture-perfect long red hair, but a photo of a skunk.

"A skunk?" Madison said with disbelief. She covered her face with her hands.

Egg chuckled. "Really smells, doesn't it?"

Madison frowned. "Not the time to be funny."

"Now I think we need to take this seriously, you two. I think I have to let Principal Bernard know what is happening now."

"Mrs. Wing, I swear we triple-checked all the pages, the scans, the HTML code you and Mr. Lynch showed us how to input. I swear."

Mrs. Wing nodded. "I'm sure you did."

Drew walked in on the mess. He couldn't believe his eyes. "Oh no. Look! Ivy's a skunk, Maddie."

"No kidding, smart guy!" Egg said.

"Oh, Mrs. WIng I know that I double-checked the scans yesterday, too. We all did. I just don't—"

"Madison, I don't blame you. I don't blame any of you. But now this is a problem I have to handle from here." Mrs. Wing took over.

Madison stared at the monitor. Seeing the skunk on the page meant that her ideas about Ivy being the true hacker were all wrong.

So who *was* it?

The mystery plot thickened.

"Mrs. Wing, I want to figure out who did this." Madison decided on the spot that *she* had to be the person to find the source of the problem—even if she didn't know where to begin.

"Well, I am still filing a report with the principal. But I'll let you look into this immediately. Tomorrow we'll meet again to talk about it."

The three of them spent the next half-hour eliminating Miss Skunk and putting Ivy's real photo back online.

The remainder of the day passed by in a kind of haze. At every corridor turn, at the door to each class, Madison kept expecting some kind of showdown with Ivy, just as she'd had a showdown with Aimee. No matter what Mrs. Wing said, Madison felt responsible.

Madison didn't see Ivy in science class. Did her absence mean she hadn't seen it yet and she was just late to class? Had the skunk been safely removed in

time? Or *had* she seen it and run screaming from the building?

A little after three o'clock, after the second bell, Madison got her answer. And the only screaming Ivy was ready to do was in *Madison's* direction.

"Hey, Finnster," a sarcastic voice howled from behind Madison as she went through her locker.

She twisted around.

"Madison Finn, I want an apology and I want it RIGHT NOW!" Ivy was standing there with hands on her hips, lips drawn into a mean pout.

"Apology for what?"

"For messing with my campaign. For messing with ME!" Ivy tossed her red hair back and a little fell into her eyes. She poked Madison in the breastbone with her pointy finger. "YOU can't get away with this."

"Don't touch me," Madison pushed the finger away. "Ivy, I'm trying to figure it out, I swear."

"I heard that you put a certain picture of a certain animal up on my page of the school site. I heard that you're trying to trash me and my chances to win class president. I heard—"

"Well, you heard WRONG," Madison asserted. "Who tells you this stuff?"

"None of your business!" Ivy snorted. "You don't play fair."

"I play fair, Ivy, even with you."

"What's up with *that*?" Ivy pressed her palm up

against the locker so Madison couldn't get in to get her last book. "I wonder what Principal Bernard will say about all this. I wonder what *he heard*," she added in a mocking tone of voice.

"Quit it, Ivy. I won't let you scare me."

"You are the scary one, Madison Finn."

"When did you get so mean, Ivy? You used to be so nice."

"What are you, Queen of Nice?"

The two enemies were practically spitting on each other. A few lockers away, a small crowd was gathering.

"Madison Finn, you don't know what nice is."

"Ivy Daly, you don't know what *friendship* is."

"Don't be stupid."

"*You're* stupid."

"No, you are."

"Liar," Madison said without thinking.

"You are the liar," Ivy yelled.

"Takes one to know one."

"You're the one who backstabs and runs away from friends."

"Shut up!" Madison felt her skin get all clammy. This had become so personal all of a sudden. It wasn't really about the skunk anymore and they both knew it. Suddenly Madison felt like she was back in third grade with her scratchy kneesocks and braids.

Ivy yelled a little louder. "So why should I believe *anything* you ever say?"

"Believe whatever you want," Madison shot back. "I didn't put the picture up there. Go ahead and tell the principal. I don't care."

"I think I *WILL* tell!"

"You know what, Ivy? You're no skunk. You're a RAT!"

"Well, you're a—" For a split second it seemed that Ivy didn't have a response. She gave Madison an evil stare and took a deep breath. "You're a *COW*."

One of the bystanders laughed out loud and suddenly Madison got very nervous. She looked up at Ivy.

"Well?" Ivy barked. "No more answers from the brainiac?"

Madison had to run. She cut to the left and took off down the hall.

"Crybaby!" Ivy shouted after her. By now the rest of the kids had dispersed. Ivy turned in the opposite direction. She had won.

Madison disappeared into the girls' bathroom around the corner. She couldn't face anyone right now, especially not eighth graders milling about in the hall. She couldn't even look into her own reflection in the bathroom mirror.

She wished Bigwheels were here right now to tell her what to do.

```
From: MadFinn
To: Bigwheels
Subject: What Do I Do?
Date: Fri 15 Sept 3:19 PM
```

Hello? Are you out there? I haven't heard from you.

Hasn't been a great week. HELP!

I'm @ the school media center right now. I have an English paper due and I have not even picked the book I'm writing a report on. Can you help with that? Help (x100) is basically what I need on that and some other stuff I'd rather IM you or chat about.

Please write again. Is something wrong? I'm worried.

Yours till the ping pongs,
MadFinn

p.s. Thanks in advance.

Chapter 9

In the corner of the Waterses' living room, Chet, Egg, and Drew were firing weapons onto a target—a computer target. They were busy playing *Commando Missiles*, a new CD-ROM that Chet had bought the day before.

"Hit it! Yes! No! Hit it!" Egg was jumping up and down. Drew had control of the joystick.

Chet groaned. "You shoulda cut out. Now you're gonna die, man."

Drew looked a little flustered. "I don't even know how to play this. Aaaah!"

"WOULD YOU GUYS PLEASE SHUT UP?" Fiona screamed. "We're trying to get organized over here."

"Egg, are you gonna help with posters?" Aimee asked. "Or are you chained to your computer games?"

"Yeah, I'm thinking of a slogan."

"Thinking of a slogan?" Madison laughed out loud. "Tell us."

Egg put his hands on his hips. "Well, how about 'Aimee Rocks'?"

Aimee made a raspberry noise with her lips. "That's my vote on that slogan. Are you serious?"

Egg made a serious face. "Always, Aimee."

"How about *that*?" Fiona spoke up. "For a slogan, I mean."

"What?"

"'Always Aimee.'" Fiona thought it was a great idea.

Aimee wasn't too crazy about any of the slogans on the list so far.

Aimee's Awesome
Aimee 4-Ever
Aimee Aces the Prez!
Have You Voted Aimee Yet?
Aimee's Alright!
Awake and Aimee
Ready, Aimee, Fire
Honest Aimee

Everyone had all gone to the Waterses' house for snacks and poster preparation. It was the end of a long week and Fiona, Chet, Egg, Drew, Aimee, and Madison were rolling up their sleeves to make Aimee's last-minute round of campaign posters.

They needed more to hang in the hallways for the week of the election. It was time to get out the poster board and Magic Markers.

The other two candidates, Montrell and Tommy, had hung a few posters here and there, but *no one* could match Ivy's poster invasion.

"I think we should put posters up all over the gym, too. I mean *all over*. Maybe we should try gym sayings or something," Aimee said. "Like 'Vote Aimee: It's a slam dunk!'"

"That's cool," Drew said.

"You really think so?" Aimee sounded happy to hear that Drew liked her ideas.

"And the library too, don't forget," Madison reminded them of another place where students would be sure to *read* the posters.

"What about the dance studio?" Chet spoke up. "You're a dancer, right?"

"Everyone in the dance troupe says they're voting for me already," Aimee said.

"Cookies!" Mrs. Waters came into the living room all of a sudden with a tray of homemade gingersnaps. Everyone grabbed as many cookies as they could stuff into their mouths.

"Not too many at once, guys!" Mrs. Waters said.

Twenty gingersnaps each and twenty minutes later, Chet, Drew, and Egg got bored with the slogans and word games. They went back to playing *Commando Missiles*.

Then the doorbell rang.

"Hey, Maddie, can you get that?" Fiona yelled out. Madison was closest to the door.

Madison opened it quickly without thinking. She had cookie crumbs all down the front of her shirt.

"Finnster!"

She jumped. Behind Door Number One was none other than Hart Jones.

"Madison, what are *YOU* doing here?" Hart asked.

"There's a bunch of us here making posters for the election. You know, for Aimee." She took a breath. "You wanna help out?"

"Maybe another time—hey, what's with the cookies?" He chuckled.

Madison brushed off the crumbs and gave him a dirty look.

"Sorry," Hart said sheepishly.

"Okay, then." Madison fumbled for something else to say. "Okay?"

"Yeah, okay, then." Hart fumbled too.

"Yeah, well . . ." Madison grinned and turned to go back inside.

"Finnster?" Hart took a step to follow her, but by then Chet had air-boxed his way over to the door, screeching, "Watch it, Jones! Watch it! J-O-N-E-S!"

"See ya, Finnster," Hart was still calling after Madison.

"Feeeenster?" Chet mimicked him.

All four boys vanished outside together to shoot some hoops.

As Fiona shut the door, Aimee wailed, "What about the posters? Who's gonna finish up?"

"We are!" Fiona laughed. "Did you really expect those guys to do anything real? They were total loads, as always. Especially Chet."

Aimee curled up on the sofa. "Hey, you guys, I have a confession to make."

"What?" Fiona asked curiously.

Aimee tilted her head back. "I think I like someone. A little."

Madison rushed over to the floor next to her. "Who? Oh Aimee, who? Why didn't you tell me?"

Aimee rolled her eyes. "Because."

"Who is it?" Fiona asked. "Is it Hart Jones, because he's pretty cute—"

"No, you can't!" Madison blurted out.

Aimee and Fiona looked at her in silence, stunned.

"What do you mean, 'No!' Maddie?"

Madison chewed on her lip—and lied through her teeth. "No, of course not! He's a freak. He always calls me Finnster. Please. No, I only yelled that because—"

Aimee and Fiona nodded. "Okay, Maddie. If you say so."

"I don't like *anyone* and no one likes me. That's okay with me," Madison said.

"You know, we should finish election posters," Aimee said, "before it gets too late. We can talk about boys later." She had brought up the subject suddenly and now she suddenly wanted to change it.

"But you didn't tell us. . . . Who do you like, Aimee?" Fiona wanted to know.

"Well, I dunno. I don't really like anyone."

"Okay." Fiona gave up. "Then I don't like anyone either."

"That is such a lie! You're crushing on Egg, you admitted it!"

Fiona smiled. "Egg who?"

The three girls laughed.

Hart

Rude Awakening: Crushing can be hazardous to your health.

OK, so I saw him this morning in the library media center. Is it to be or not to be??? He was wearing a nice brown sweater. I swear I don't know how it is possible that I like him. I know I do. I like Hart. I CANNOT TELL ANYONE. Aimee would die. Fiona would probably say "Way to Go," but then she'd find something wrong with him. Friends do that a lot.

Of course I saw him today at Fiona's too. And it feels like I ate something funny just to think or talk about it. The

little hairs on my arms all stand up. Is that weird? Part of what makes Hart hard to handle is that he can be so *mean* to me. Does that make any sense that a guy who likes you would dis you? He was ok @ Fiona's actually, but around other school peeps he is obnoxious with a capital O.

I just don't get boys. One minute they're so nice and the next minute they're so not. Does crushing on someone also mean MY heart is gonna get squashed?

Back at the Gillespies' later on, Madison tried to finish up her science homework before the weekend. Of course it was hard to get through any science assignment without thinking about Poison Ivy, her esteemed lab partner, but Madison tried. She typed up all her lab notes from class.

As soon as she clicked off her laptop, Madison sat on the floor so Aimee could french-braid her hair. Aimee was the best braider *ever*—even better than Egg's older sister Mariah, who had hair all the way down to her waist.

"Maddie," Aimee said as she pulled the hair back, "I hope you find out tomorrow what loser is ruining your Web site. That is so messed about what happened with Ivy's picture."

"Yeah, it stinks."

A second later Madison realized what she had said. The whole *skunk* thing stank. The two friends laughed. Madison started to laugh so much she almost forgot about the election Web site. . . .

Almost.

"Stop twitching," Aimee said. "Hold still."

"You're *pulling*!"

"Not me. It's you. HOLD STILL."

Madison had too many tangles.

"I still have to write my campaign assembly speech, Maddie. Can you help me do it before the assembly?"

"You're gonna be great, Aim, I know it. You're not worried, are you?"

Aimee shrugged and twisted Madison's hair into the tail end of the braid, while Phinnie curled into Madison's lap. He wouldn't stop kissing her hand and every time he did, Madison saw the little black stripe on his pink tongue. This dog was so cute. Cute and homesick, too. Madison could feel it. When she scritched behind Phin's ears, he hummed like a motor.

"Madison?" Mrs. Gillespie knocked softly on Aimee's door and peered inside. "There's a phone call for you."

It was almost eleven.

"Hello, honey." Dad's voice sounded like a low hum over the phone line, too. He was calling to check in because he hadn't heard anything in a day or so. "Is everything good?"

Madison yawned. "Yeah, I guess."

"I was thinking all day today about you but I got stuck in this meeting and—"

"Daddy?" He had been talking about his latest business venture, when Madison interrupted him.

"I lied."

"What did you say, honey?"

"I'm really not so good. Well, I'm better now, but school is just really tough."

"Oh, Maddie, why didn't you tell me? Should I speak to someone—"

"No, I don't want to make a big deal out of it or anything."

"Okay, well, you know, maybe you should leave the Gillespies' and come stay with me for the next day or so. Your mom gets back when?"

"Soon."

"Why don't you come over until she gets back?"

"Is Stephanie there?" Madison asked.

Dad took a moment to respond. "Uh, no. Why would you think that?"

"Because. You guys seem pretty close already. I just imagined that she was moving in or something major."

"Maddie, *no*." Dad put all the stress on the word "no."

Madison wanted to see him, but the truth was that she wanted to stay with Aimee *more* right now.

"Daddy, I think I'm just gonna stay here so I can cheer on Aimee in the election, okay? And Phinnie's

here, so I'm okay. I can see you on Sunday, maybe. Is that okay? You probably want to do stuff with Stephanie then, right?"

"Maddie," Dad crooned, "what's with all this Stephanie stuff? You know honey, *you're* the apple of my—"

"Eye." Of course, Madison knew. She was just playing it safe. Just in case Stephanie *did* show up unannounced.

Just like that, the conversation was over.

Dad didn't argue with Madison's decision to stay at Aimee's rather than go. He wasn't an arguing kind of guy. If Mom wanted something she'd ask for it twelve times until she got it. Dad was different. He gave up easier. Of course, that made him easier to understand, too. In many ways, Dad was probably the only "boy" in Madison's life who was the least bit predictable. He was the only boy she understood.

She couldn't say *that* about Drew, or Egg, and especially not Hart Jones.

Madison didn't get Hart one itty-bitty bit.

Chapter 10

"Hey, mmwill you help me fix mmup my mmam-paign speech tonight?" Aimee asked through a mouthful of brown rice. "I have some ideas but I could mmreally use your super-brain. I mmam so worried about the mmassembly."

Madison looked down at her lukewarm vegetarian burrito and shrugged without taking any kind of bite whatsoever. "Okay. Sure."

It was Sunday. She'd spent the weekend raking leaves in the Gillespie yard, working on her English essay, and playing Age of Empires online with Egg. (She wasn't very good—but then, Egg beat almost everyone.) Madison had a page of vocabulary words to memorize and now she had to help craft an election speech?

Madison didn't want to do *anything* with the

election right now, not even to help her best friend in the universe. She couldn't get the gila monster and skunk episodes out of her head.

From: MadFinn
To: Bigwheels
Subject: This Weekend
Date: Sun 17 Sept 3:53 PM

Where r u?????? How is your life? I am living a life of HELP! Did you get my other emails????? I was waiting for a response. I hope you r ok.

Weekends are like Roswell or Twilight Zone and I can tell you why. There are these moments in time when people sort of float in and out of your life and set your head spinning a little. Do you know what I mean? Here is my proof:

1. Dad was supposed to come by this weekend to take me and Phinnie (my dog) out for a long aftenoon. But then he couldn't at the last minute because of work and he said he was so sorry. I say something came up with this new girlfriend he has.

2. I saw one of the other election candidates @ the mall, Tommy and some friends who were loud and not so nice to me. He thinks he's so cute but he is wicked fake. And his friend Brendan is even worse. He called me stupid. Boys can be such DORKS.

3. My Mom is still in Paris.
I think I have now told you my entire life right now. I am mainly checking in because I haven't written much and haven't heard from you. You give good advice, did I ever tell you that? So please do. Okay? Maybe we can have another online conversation one of these days? I remember last week we met in the room GOFISHY.

Your IM name is the same, right? Mine's MadFinn like everything. C ya.

Yours till the candle sticks,
MadFinn

No sooner had she hit SEND, than Madison saw her mailbox icon blinking. She and Bigwheels had sent e-mails to each other at *exactly* the same time.

From: Bigwheels
To: MadFinn
Subject: I Wonder
Date: Sun 17 Sept 3:53 PM

I had a cold and wasn't on the computer for almost three days. I had 16 e-mails when I logged on today. Three were from YOU.
I hope you are not mad at me. Well, I know you are, MadFinn, but you'll just get over it, right?

How is the election going? I wonder about other things too. I know you asked me about boys before. Are you going out with someone?

Did I ever tell you I like fish? That's why I first joined bigfishbowl.com. Well, 2 of my very own tropical fish died this weekend. My father says they caught my cold. I think he wanted me to feel better about it but I don't.

I wish you would write me again, too.

Yours till the dandy lions,

Bigwheels

Madison turned on her IM Buddy List to see if maybe Bigwheels was online right now. But she wasn't. *That was weird.*

Another name popped up, though.

```
INSTA-MESSAGE to MadFinn
<Wetwinz>: Helloooooooo Maddie!
```

It was Fiona, also known as Wetwinz.

Fiona and Aimee didn't know about Madison's online friend Bigwheels, but they did know about the bigfishbowl.com site. It was kind of hard to keep that a secret. It was the most popular chat site at Far Hills Junior High.

Aimee never went on the computer because she thought Insta-Messages were annoying. Aimee didn't chat much. She thought why type when you could just talk? Wasn't it way easier to just pick up the phone? Aimee didn't even have a screen name.

Fiona had only started her online chatting. Her Mom had been nervous about giving her permission to do things online before junior high had started. Now, she decided to give Fiona and Chet online access.

```
INSTA-MESSAGE REPLY to Wetwinz
<MadFinn>: Hey you. Meet me in room
STARFISH.
```

Madison liked the way that sounded, so she picked it as her private chatroom destination.

<Wetwinz>: What is happening is something wrong?
<MadFinn>: I'm fine
<Wetwinz>: At my house Fri. you seemed a littlebummmed out 2 me
<MadFinn>: not really
<Wetwinz>: How was today
<MadFinn>: I had squishy vege burritos 4 dinner!
<Wetwinz>: LOL

Fiona had heard daily updates on the wacky dinners Madison was eating—and not eating—while staying with Aimee and her family.

<MadFinn>: yuk but seriously
<Wetwinz>: is school bumming you out maddie???
<MadFinn>: not school no
<Wetwinz>: then what??? I can tell don't lie 2 me
<MadFinn>: remember that fight onFriday???
<Wetwinz>: Ivy???
<MadFinn>: Y
<Wetwinz>: IMS! U know Chet told me too he saw and heard it did you know?

<MadFinn>: that is sooo embarrassing. He did? Who else
<Wetwinz>: AFK

Fiona was Away From the Keyboard.

Madison scrolled back up to reread what they'd said so far.

<Wetwinz>: sorry!! stupid Chet walked in just then
<MadFinn>: maybe we should talk F2F in skool
<Wetwinz>: r u bummed because Ivy is mean?
<Wetwinz>: I'm ur friend . . .

Madison grinned and nodded at the computer screen.

Fiona was a *good* friend, too.

<Wetwinz>: r u there?
<MadFinn>: THX, F
<Wetwinz>: n e time
<MadFinn>: <Hugs back> (())**
<Wetwinz>: c u tomorrow in class?
<Wetwinz>: <:D

The next morning, Madison left for school extra early so she could tally and present the latest poll on the school site. After the conversation with Fiona, she decided once and for all that she really could

leave the whole Ivy episode behind. She could get back to her computer duties and get back into gear.

There was no need to feel embarrassed, either. Madison had real friends where it really mattered. Not only that, but today the Web site looked sabotage free, thankfully. And the online poll taker was working perfectly.

As of today's tally, girls *ruled.*

9/18 CURRENT STANDINGS:
What candidate will do the most for Far Hills?
48% Ivy Daly
32% Aimee Gillespie
12% Montrell Morris
8% Thomas Kwong

Unfortunately, girls named Ivy ruled better than girls named Aimee. But Madison told herself to ignore that gigantic lead. She had to focus on the good stuff, not the bad stuff. Aimee still had a chance to win.

The bell for homeroom rang.

In the middle of roll call, Madison realized she had done all her homework for the day except science. Why hadn't she finished her science reading? She'd have to sneak into the girls' room before class to skim-read the chapters. Sometimes Madison would hide out in a stall to finish math problems or

read through essays before class started. That way she could show up a little late and say she was "in the bathroom."

Unfortunately, as Madison discovered that afternoon, the science reading had a lot of new vocabulary. And Madison read so fast the chapter wasn't making much sense.

There would probably be a pop quiz today, too.

It was several moments after the bell had rung, and still Mr. Danehy had not shown up. Some kid poked his head into the classroom.

"Mr. D's stuck in a meeting and he'll be late."

The class began humming. From all corners of the room, different conversations started up like chain saws.

Bzzzzzzzzzzzzzzzzzzzzzzzz.

"Hey, Finnster," Hart whispered loudly across class. "You okay? I mean, considering . . ."

Madison made a face. "Yeah," she said. Of course she was okay. Why would he ask her that? Considering *what*?

"You have a lotta nerve," Rose Thorn said not-so-nicely from her seat at the front of the room.

Another kid mumbled, "Show-off."

Madison turned toward her seat.

What were they talking about?

"Nice Web site!" a boy from the back of the room yelled. The rest of the class laughed, especially, Poison Ivy.

"Now, settle down." Chet banged on Mr. Danehy's desk, pretending to be the teacher. "I will not stand for these reee-diculous deee-sruptions!"

Hart was laughing so hard his face turned all pink.

Were they laughing at her?

"Hey, Maddie," Phony Joanie called out. "How does it feel to be a screen star?"

Madison shook her head. "What are you all talking about?" She flipped through her textbook frantically, trying to ignore everyone and study more.

Ivy let out a big "HAH!" She was doodling "class president" all over her science book cover.

"Ivy, is there something going on that I don't know about?"

Ivy adjusted her skirt and crossed her legs. "Oh, Madison, poor you. Don't you get it?"

The tone in Ivy's voice told Madison that something was *definitely* wrong.

Madison knew it must have to do with the Web site. "Is this about the skunk again?"

"What do you think?" Ivy said.

Madison wanted to run to the nearest computer just to check and make sure the skunk wasn't back again, but no sooner had she stood up when Mr. Danehy came into the classroom. He was waving papers in front of him.

"Pop quiz, kids!"

Everyone let out a dejected "Awwww" even though they had all seen the quiz coming.

Madison clutched at her throat. Panic was working its way up, faster now than before. She felt hot all over. She had to get to a computer—NOW.

Every bit of classroom chatter sounded ominous.

"Messed . . . Web . . . she . . . joke."

She only could catch a few words here and there, but she was sure that they were targeted directly at her.

"Mad . . . Wing . . . site . . . can't . . . bad . . . Madison."

There was more whispering and rustling as Mr. Danehy passed out the quizzes—and funny stares all around.

Madison looked down at the pop quiz. It was a gray blur.

"Class, you will have fifteen minutes to complete . . ." Mr. Danehy explained what the quiz was about.

"Gee, Madison." Ivy leaned in close to her. "Don't you have the scientific data to fill in this quiz?" Ivy laughed softly and twirled a piece of hair around her finger, waiting for Madison to take the bait.

"Ivy, your idea of scientific data," Madison said, "is a scientist who likes to go on dates!"

It was a good answer, but it didn't count for much. Ivy was still laughing.

Madison's skin flushed. Her neck was sweating.

She could feel the room starting to spin a little.

And when Hart bellowed, "Way to go, Finnster!" Madison *really* lost it.

"Yeah, GO Finnster!" Ivy cried a little louder. "GO take a look at the election Web site."

Everyone got very quiet. Even Mr. Danehy stopped explaining for a split second. Dozens of eyes landed on Madison's hot skin.

She wanted to scream. She wanted to cry. She wanted to . . .

RUN.

"Miss Finn?" Mr. Danehy was surprised and more than a little rattled. Science teachers were not typically trained to deal with freaking-out seventh-grade girls. "Miss Finn? Are you all right?"

Madison bolted out of her chair.

What was she doing?

She ran out the door, down the hallway, down past the girls' room, past the hall monitor, down the stairs, all the way to Mrs. Wing's classroom.

No one was following her. She gasped for air.

Feelings are like fuel that jet-propel you into places and situations you don't even expect.

"What's wrong?" Mrs. Wing asked as Madison rushed into the technology lab, breathless. "You're purple!"

Madison's felt the tears and anger making her face all blotchy.

"We have to check the Web site, Mrs. Wing," Madison gasped again.

"Oh dear, I think you need to see the nurse," Mrs. Wing said.

But Madison had already logged on to the computer station and punched the right keys.

"Madison, I really think you should slow down and tell me what it is that you are looking for," Mrs. Wing added.

"Oh no." Madison turned to look up at her teacher.

Mrs. Wing stared back at the monitor.

There was the home page for the school's election site—but with one big difference. The photo of the *school* was gone.

In its place, there was a picture of Madison Finn with three little words: FINN FOR PREZ.

Chapter 11

Madison learned later on that day that thanks to her crying and fleeing, Mr. Danehy had lost all sense of order in his classroom and thereby decided to forget about the science pop quiz. So what had started out as the most embarrassing thing that could ever happen to anyone, ironically ended up winning Madison more *friends*. Her entire science class was ready to high-five her, as if Madison's freak show had somehow turned into the perfect pop-quiz-blocking method of all time.

Nothing made any sense anymore.

"Are you okay, Maddie?" Drew asked her later on in Mrs. Wing's tech lab. Madison was fixated on the screen image: FINN FOR PREZ. She couldn't even delete it this time.

"What IS that?" Drew asked.

The photo of Madison kept shifting in and out of focus. Mrs. Wing walked over to the classroom phone and dialed the Administration office.

"Do you think someone is doing this on purpose?" Drew wondered out loud.

"Don't you? Or maybe it's just a coincidence that they put FINN FOR PREZ? I don't think so."

"Principal Bernard is coming up right now, you two," Mrs. Wing said as she clicked a few more keys. Madison watched Mrs. Wing jump from computer screen to screen, checking in once again on all of the other pages. Madison wanted to be like her almost as much as she wanted to be like Mom. Mrs. Wing was so smart, Madison thought again. She wanted to be smart, and wear iridescent earrings, and sip hot coffee in the morning.

Madison wanted a lot of things.

"Where is Mr. Diaz?" Mrs. Wing asked. She was smart, but she was also very annoyed. She didn't like the way this computer prank was turning out. It was jeopardizing the entire school election.

No sooner had she asked the question than Egg appeared.

"Sorry I'm late, Mrs.—check that out!" Egg spied the sabotaged home page screen. "Maddie, you're on the home page! Hey, Mrs. Wing, do you—?"

"Walter, would you please just sit down. This is a serious problem."

Egg was surprised by Mrs. Wing's stern tone of

voice. His crush had just dealt him a crushing blow.

"Walter, take a seat please," Mrs. Wing repeated.

He collapsed into a chair. "She hates me," Egg whispered to Drew.

Meanwhile, Madison kept trying to figure out everything Mrs. Wing had been explaining about strings and substrings and things. She looked at what was typed up on the screen.

```
Source of message.
Proxy server location.
Time of use.
```

"Is Mrs. Wing in here?"

Principal Bernard was at the classroom door. Mrs. Wing got up to speak to the principal "privately" for a moment.

Drew had a blank look on his face. He didn't want to get into trouble with the principal.

Egg wore a look of devastation. The wisecracker had cracked.

Madison tapped a few more keys and finally found the "history" of the Finn photograph flashing up on the screen. She was surprised to see that the photo had been downloaded *last Friday*.

The source of the message was a serial number.

Madison turned to Mrs. Wing, Principal Bernard, and the rest of the room. She grinned proudly. "I know where the photo was sent from."

"Madison?" Mrs. Wing smiled. "You do? Well, good for you. You were paying close attention, I see."

"Miss Finn, I am impressed," Principal Bernard said. "Does this mean you can tell us who the prankster is?"

"Way to go, Maddie," Drew pumped his fist in the air.

Egg looked up, too. "Can you really tell who did it just by looking—"

"Maybe!" Madison nodded. "The photo here was sent from a computer up on the sixth floor," she explained. "See, I figured out that each computer has its own code based on its location."

Mrs. Wing was smiling wider now, as if she was *proud*. She gave Principal Bernard a sidelong glance.

"So computer 611FH is the only unit with a six in the code," Madison continued. "The older main building is the only building with a sixth floor. And the only computer on the sixth floor is in the library."

Mrs. Wing was genuinely impressed.

"Whoa," Egg said. "You figured all that out from looking at that code?"

Principal Bernard piped up. "Don't they keep logs so people who use computers have to sign in and out of the media center?"

Mrs. Wing held up her hands as if to say, "This is your ball, Madison Finn. Run with it."

So Madison ran all the way up to the sixth floor.

She wondered what she'd find in the log. Maybe the culprit was Rose Thorn or Phony Joanie?

Mr. Books was just closing up the library as they climbed the stairs.

"Hello, there. What is the big rush?"

"We may have a little computer problem happening from your station up here, Mr. Books. I know it's hard to believe, but quite true. Miss Finn here seems to have found the source."

The library computer logbook was laid out on a wooden table near the station. Madison rushed over to it, followed by Drew, Egg, Mrs. Wing, Mr. Books, and Principal Bernard.

"Okay." Madison searched in a frenzy. She flipped back to Friday's entries. "I know the download happened at ten-forty P.M. So, that means I'll find it right here."

Madison ran her finger down the list of sign-in names—and stopped.

She took a step backward.

"Who is it?" Mrs. Wing asked with concern. "Madison, is it someone you know?"

"Worse," Madison groaned. "Drew, look."

There was nothing listed for a 10:40 download. There was no one in school then. No one had used the computer over the weekend, either.

But on the list was a very familiar name.

Madison Finn.

"I guess that's not who you expected to see, right?" Egg said.

"Very funny," Madison grunted.

Drew elbowed Egg in the side.

Everyone else was tongue-tied.

And Madison was right back where she had started.

Which was, basically, *nowhere*.

The Conspiracy

Rude Awakening: Sometimes it's easier to believe your enemies than your friends.

I am at the center of a Far Hills Junior High conspiracy, I swear. Of course, I shouldn't be talking about it so much. That's like whammying myself to have even worse luck. But I can't help it.

When Aimee got back from her dance troupe tonight I told her everything. She almost died when she heard. She said it was like a REAL conspiracy. Like a movie. I sent mom another e-mail too and told her about it, since she is the movie person, after all. And Fiona and Bigwheels know too, of course. I couldn't leave them out.

At least this election Web site is only

accessible at school. But I don't think I will ever recover from the embarrassment.

That evening, Maddie set up her laptop in a corner of Aimee's bedroom to do her homework. But she just didn't feel like studying. What was the point in attempting to solve a tough math equation when she couldn't even figure out who had invaded the school Web site?

Madison wanted to work more on her files. She wanted to get to the bottom of the Web site mystery. She considered the suspects.

Poison Ivy Enemy #1
Rose and Joanie
The other candidates: Montrell? Tommy?
Definite not Aimee, Egg, Mrs. Wing, or Fiona
Hart Jones?

After she typed Hart's name for the first time Madison got a little distracted. She entered it a few more times.

Hart Hart Hart HART hart
Maddie + Hart
Madison Jones

When Madison realized what she was *really* typing, she pressed DELETE. What if her file got into the wrong hands?

Plus, Gramma Helen had always told Maddie

never to write anything that she wouldn't want someone else to see. "Think before you ink, Madison," Gramma would say.

Madison figured the same rule had to be true about stuff keyed in on the computer. She didn't want *anyone* to know the way she felt about the guy who called her Finnster. It was way too embarrassing.

When Mrs. Gillespie screeched from downstairs, "Frittatas! Come and get it!" Madison wasn't sure what to expect.

Would tonight's dinner selection be better or worse than the sand or vegetables from the nights before?

Phinnie was, of course, waiting in the dining room. He was such a little beggar. Madison poured kibble into the PHIN FOOD dish, and he muscled in for his chow. Blossom howled too. Together they looked like they were performing a doggy comedy routine.

Dinner was unusually quiet. Mr. Gillespie made dinner conversation with the "girls," since none of his four sons was eating at home tonight. Things were definitely less interesting without the boys around.

"Aimee, have you written your campaign speech yet?"

Aimee chuckled. "I'm working on it, Daddy."

Madison added, "It's going to be great, Mr. Gillespie."

"Maddie's gonna help me write it, Daddy."

"Yeah," Madison continued, "Aimee's saying really smart stuff. Better than Ivy Daly anyway."

Aimee nodded. "That's for sure."

"Ivy Daly? You mean Jack Daly's girl?" Mr. Gillespie said. "Now, weren't you girls all friends at one point?"

"Only like a million and a half years ago, Daddy!" Aimee swallowed a mouthful of lentils. They were little brown beans piled high on a platter in the middle of the table, a platter that Madison was avoiding at all costs. Maddie opted for extra helpings of potatoes instead.

"I could have sworn you three were still friends." Mr. Gillespie was perplexed.

Madison thought about how funny it was that parents could fall so far out of the loop of friends and acquaintances sometimes. There was a time in life once when everyone's moms and dads knew everyone's friends, those friends' parents, and all the friends' pets. But things were different now. Way different.

"We were friends in elementary school," Madison said to clarify things. "When we were kids."

"Oh," Mr. Gillespie said, surprised. "And now you are—?"

"In junior high, Dad. Gimme a break. We are not babies anymore. Things are just different."

"Watch your tone, Aimee, please," Mrs. Gillespie reprimanded her.

Aimee sulked a little.

"Madison, I thought Ivy Daly always seemed like such a nice girl," Mrs. Gillespie continued, "and you used to have so much fun together."

Madison laughed out loud. "Well, you should see Poison Ivy now."

"Poison *who*?" Mrs. Gillespie was lost. "What did you call her?"

Mr. Gillespie just shook his head. "You girls change friends like you change the cable-TV channels. I can't keep up."

"But Maddie and I are still here," Aimee crooned. She stood up and danced her way into the kitchen with the dirty dishes.

"I stand corrected then," Mr. Gillespie said. "You only change *some* of the channels."

After dinner, while Aimee watched a TV show about jazz dancers, Madison went looking for an e-mail from Bigwheels in her mailbox.

Her heart leaped.

Maddie's bigfishbowl.com friend had written back sooner than soon—as requested.

Phin jumped onto the bed next to Madison. Since her orange laptop was taking up *his* usual spot on her lap, Phinnie snuggled into Madison's side, snorting and scratching at the sheets to make just the right spot for his little body.

From: Bigwheels
To: MadFinn
Subject: Poem and other stuff
Date: Mon 18 Sept 9:24 AM

Yes I am writing again! I'm writing from MY school media center. Ha! I decided that the best way to cheer you up was to send you a poem I wrote when I was feeling like a total outsider when it seemed like the world was after me and against me. It happens to everyone I think. People can be so mean and hurtful. Even though my poem says so, you are not alone!!! NO WAY! You know that these poems are not how I am always, right? I feel good mostly. But when I don't it just comes out like here. 'Bye.

Frown

I am bugged by some of the people
Just who do they think they are?
I am crushed at school near and far
Sometimes I feel it like a squeeze
that won't end
I want to stop the crush
I want to have a normal friend
I like to talk on the phone
It keeps me from being alone

If you are having a hard time too
Do not worry just tell someone
about it
Like your mom or teacher too
Don't ever let anyone get you down
And most of all don't frown

Write back soon and tell me what
happens with the election this week.
Bye.

Yours till the gum drops,

Bigwheels

As soon as Madison read the poem, she knew that maybe she could believe this friend—*way* more than any of her enemies. Bigwheels' e-mail energized her.

Tomorrow Maddie could find out who the culprit was, and she could make the election Web site work.

Then Mrs. Wing would *really* be impressed.

Chapter 12

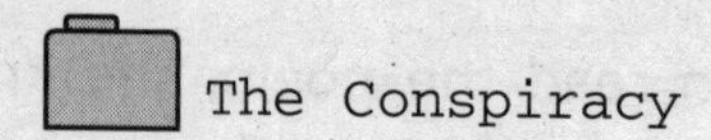

The Conspiracy

Rude Awakening: Objects on the calendar are closer than they appear.

Two more days left.

Suddenly the election is here and I am no closer to finding the computer hacker than I was yesterday or the day before that. Of course I never wanted to be Nancy Drew, but I could do better than THIS. I always guess the wrong rooms when I play Clue and hit all the dead ends in all the video games. Sometimes it's like all the signs are here, there, and everywhere and I'm wandering aimlessly in the middle of it all.

And I'm Aimee-less, too. At least for

now. She's off dancing somewhere as usual. I'm slumming in the technology lab. Mrs. Wing isn't saying much.

I haven't seen much of Ivy. Right up until yesterday I actually thought she could still be guilty of the Web site problems STILL. Esp. when the FINN FOR PREZ thing came up. But now I know that's not so.

It's kind of bad, because if Ivy *had* been the one responsible and I had proved she *was* the one responsible then I could know for sure right know that Aimee Anne Gillespie would win the election.

Madison couldn't stop thinking either, about conspiracies and homework and ice cream.

"Maddie!" Drew ran up to her later in the hallway after lunch.

"Drew, where were you?"

"In the other building . . ." He coughed. "I had to find—you—to show . . ." He stopped to catch his breath.

"Drew, what's going on? Is this some kind of freaky joke again? Because if it is, it really isn't funny—"

Drew shoved a folded-up piece of paper in front of Madison. "I think you should read this."

Madison made a face as she grabbed the paper. She wasn't sure what kind of game he was playing. All week long Drew had been everywhere she was,

like a computer virus himself. He and Egg both.

The page was all scribbles and hard to read, but Madison could make out a few key phrases. She decoded its message.

```
Network passwords: CSXRUNNING
                   ELECTIONBASE
                   ELECT891WING
File/words:        A:/GILA.BMP
                   A:/SKUN.BMP
                   A:/FINN.BMP
                   A:/WING.BMP
                   FLASH: TOMMY RULES
MF(locker combo)   658
```

"Where," Madison gulped. "Where did you get this?" She almost dropped the torn sheet onto the floor.

Drew explained, "I was sitting there in social studies class and—"

"THAT'S MY LOCKER COMBINATION!" Madison shouted. She pointed to the note, shocked by its discovery. "Did you hear what I said?"

Drew nodded politely. "I think the whole hallway heard you."

Madison quickly glanced over at the locker banks to make sure no one was listening or watching the two of them anymore.

"Pretty bad, huh?" Drew rocked from foot to foot.

"*Where* did you get this?"

"Like I said, I was in social studies class and these kids got up to leave and—"

"Drew! Someone has written down all the files and the combination to my locker and the network codes assigned by the school and Mrs. Wing. This is MAJOR."

Drew nodded.

"This is like get-suspended-from-school MAJOR."

Drew nodded again.

"Don't just stand there—tell me what happened!" Madison said.

Drew sighed a heavy sigh (since he'd been trying to get a word in edgewise for the last five minutes). He had seen a group of kids hanging out before class with Tommy Kwong, one of the other candidates. They all sat together in social studies. This one kid dropped the sheet of paper on his way out of class.

"He didn't feel it or see it or stop to pick it up," Drew added. "So I picked it up for him. It was Brendan Lo."

"Who's Brendan Lo?" Madison cried when she heard his name. After a moment, she realized maybe he was in her science class. Or was it English? She couldn't be sure.

"You don't know him?" Drew asked. "That's weird. Why would he—"

"I know!" Madison cried. "Tommy's friend. The one who was a jerk at the mall. Whoa."

Madison wondered why Brendan was stupid enough to let himself be discovered. How could someone who had been so computer smart, who had gone to all the trouble to hide his tracks, even signing her name, and who had been so clever about scanning photos and sabotaging the site . . . would then let himself get caught with a handwritten note? Madison remembered her Gramma Helen's old saying once again: *Think before you ink*. It was truer than true right now.

Drew adjusted the paper and pointed to the page where it listed files: GILA (for the lizard), SKUN (for the skunk), FINN (for Madison), and then WING.

"Do you see that? He was even gonna put up something online with Mrs. Wing's picture or something. That's what that means, right?"

Madison slid down the wall and hugged her knees.

This was it.

This was the proof Madison needed to show that *she* had not been responsible in any way for what had gone wrong on the Web site.

It was too good to be true.

"This isn't some kind of joke, is it, Drew?"

"What?" Drew wrinkled his forehead. "Are *you* kidding?"

"I mean, you and Egg aren't playing some mean trick on me, are you? Please tell me this note is real and that this kid Brendan really wrote it."

Drew pulled the note back. "Look at this. Does it look fake? Anyway, how would we know your locker combination?"

In her heart, Madison knew Drew was telling the truth.

She rolled forward on one knee to get up and Drew extended his hand to help her. It was clammy and cool when Madison grabbed it. (She made sure Drew wasn't looking when she wiped off her hand on her pants a minute later.)

"You know, if you're gonna write a note or a letter or a journal, you'd think a person would keep it under lock and key or password-protect himself," Madison thought out loud.

"Yeah." Drew said.

"Sometimes people can be smart and stupid at the exact same time, you know?"

"Yeah." Drew shrugged. "So now what do we do?"

Madison shrugged back.

"Let's go tell Mrs. Wing. She'll know what to do."

Chapter 13

From: MadFinn
To: Bigwheels
Subject: Re: Poem and other stuff
Date: Wed 20 Sept. 3:29 PM

I have huge news so I should just spill it.

The Election Web Site Mystery is SOLVED.

Turns out that the person I told you about who was putting up all those pictures on the Web site has been suspended from school. It was this kid who was friends with one of the other candidates, Tommy. He was actually in my SCIENCE CLASS—can you believe it? He was good at

computers and wanted Tommy to win soooo much that he decided to mess with MY site. I guess Brendan wanted to embarrass me and the rest of the candidates so Tommy would be the only person left to pick.

What a weird twist. It also turns out that Brendan wasn't really a part of Tommy's crew, he just wished he was. So he figured doing this would make people like him more. It's like a bad movie of the week on TV!!! I feel so bad for this kid.

Tommy says he didn't know anything but he got pulled from the election anyhow. AND he got suspended for a week. SO harsh.

By the way, you are maybe the best poet I have ever read for a seventh grader. I mean, how are you so good? I have read your poem over and over and it is so like my life! I think the title could be "Crushed" maybe—something like that.

Please please please keep your

fingers crossed for my friend Aimee. I think she really could win this school election tomorrow w/one candidate gone now. Here's hoping.

Yours till the web links,

MadFinn

Brrrrrrrring.

By the time Thursday's 1:10 bell rang and the announcement for the election assembly came over the loudspeaker, Madison was ready to scream for joy. What would Ivy's drones Rose Thorn and Phony Joanie say when they realized their crowned princess Ivy was an L-O-S-E-R?

Classes were excused from seventh period so kids could hear the candidates' speeches and vote.

All of a sudden election day was here—and almost over.

"Attention! Students?" Principal Bernard tapped on the mike once everyone had taken seats in the auditorium. "Now, you know why we are all here?" Mr. Bernard's voice lilted so he sounded as if he was always asking a question.

Madison rolled her eyes as the lights were dimmed to show *Campaign USA*, one of those educational, how-to videos principals and social studies teachers liked to show in assembly. During the video, kids were whispering, rolling spitballs, and even

zapping messages to each other on their Cybikos (which should have been confiscated, of course, but weren't).

Madison sat up in her seat a little taller.

She could just see the top of Hart's head.

After seven minutes, when the lights went back up, Mr. Bernard cleared his throat. As always, he spoke into the microphone a little too closely.

Sqweeeeeeeeee.

Everyone cringed from the feedback.

"Now, let's announce Far Hills' candidates for class president, starting with class—"

Sqweeeeeeeeee.

Half the room clapped and stomped on the floor while the other half fanned themselves with flyers. The teachers had handed out a Far Hills Junior High Elections Guide, so everyone knew the rules, but of course no one had really read it. It was carefully attached to a printout of the candidate profiles Drew and Madison had posted on the Web. Tommy's section had been whited out.

Thankfully, Madison noticed that *these* flyers carried real photos of candidates and not pictures of lizards or skunks or Madison Finns.

Madison glanced around. A few rows back, Drew Maxwell caught her eye and waved. She waved back but then turned around again, suddenly embarrassed even though she didn't know why.

Was he smiling at her?

Madison looked back once more, but Drew was talking to Egg by then.

"As you know, we take elections at Far Hills very seriously, students," Mr. Bernard said, demanding everyone's undivided attention. "Would you please give this year's candidates your warmest welcome."

Onto the stage walked Montrell, then Poison Ivy, and Aimee.

Mrs. Wing was up near the stage fiddling with both a video camera and an instant camera. She was getting footage and photos for the Web site.

Montrell talked about how the school needed to give way less homework and throw pizza parties every Friday. Of course, he was a basketball player, so team sports was his main focus.

Madison groaned when Ivy stepped up to the microphone. It was because of the way she did it, with a sweep of her hand and a toss of her head, as if she were posing for a modeling shoot.

She acted like a winner and no one even had voted yet.

"I think Far Hills Junior High needs to bond together. We should all look out for each other and be friends." Ivy's voice was earnest but Madison knew *she* wasn't. How could the Queen of Mean call "bonding" and "friendship" her goals as class president?

Between Tommy's scandal and Ivy's attitude, Aimee *had* to win this vote.

Finally it was Aimee's turn. She pirouetted onstage, making an entrance, of course. She had written her own speech the night before with the help of Maddie, Roger, Mr. and Mrs. Gillespie, and Fiona (over the phone).

"Go, Aimee!" Fiona shouted in Madison's ear. She was crossing her fingers. She was as superstitious as Madison.

Madison clapped loudly, pinching her eyes shut just so she felt a little less nervous. This was her best friend and her best chance to stop Poison Ivy before Far Hills turned into her kingdom. Madison didn't want Junior High to turn out just like elementary school.

Aimee's voice was a little shaky at first.

"Let me begin by saying how much I love running for class prez. I love it. You guys are all really great. Doing this has given me the chance to meet lots of you and I think that being class president is so important. . . ."

She warmed up after a while. Madison was trying to pay attention throughout, but she kept getting distracted by Hart's head again each time he shifted in his seat.

"So I promise I will do my best. Even better than the rest . . ."

Madison knew this was near the end. She clapped—hard.

"Go, Aimee!"

The rest of the audience clapped, too. Even Egg and Drew circled their fists up into the air. "Woo! Woo! Woo!"

As soon as all the candidates were done, a loud kid sitting behind Madison said, "Let's get outta here already." She was painfully reminded that not everyone *really* cared as much as she did about school elections. Then again, Aimee didn't need *everyone*'s vote to win. She just needed enough to whup Ivy Daly fair and square.

Up on stage, Madison watched as Montrell shook Aimee's hand and then Ivy's. But Aimee and Ivy took a moment before they shook, smiling their plastic smiles. People who didn't know they were enemies never would have been able to tell what was *really* going on. Only Madison and Fiona knew.

The applause for candidates continued right up until the moment when the vice-presidential hopefuls came out, but Madison stopped paying attention altogether by then. She craned her neck to see what Hart was doing and kept her eyes on him.

Once all seventh-grade reps had been presented and given their chance to speak, Mr. Bernard's voice boomed again over the microphone. "Thank you, students it's time to vote." He leaned into the mike and the sharp, metallic sound of feedback blared up once again.

Sqweeeeeeeeee.

Kids covered their ears. Principal Bernard quickly

turned the microphone over to the best computer teacher on the planet, Mrs. Wing. Today she was wearing a scarf instead of beads. Madison could see multicolored numbers all over it.

"Weren't those speeches great?" She led the auditorium in another burst of applause. "Now, thank you all for paying attention to our candidates. I know most of you have visited our exciting new Web site. This year is very special because for the very first time we are voting online. I would like to take a moment to thank a few people who have helped make this election Web project possible. First, Mr. Lynch in ninth grade, who programmed the basics and got us up and running. Second, Principal Bernard who graciously gave the technology area a new proxy server over the summer. And of course to Madison Finn, Walter Diaz, and Andrew Maxwell who have worked very hard—"

"Yeah, Finnster!" Madison heard Hart yell from the front row. Everyone in the auditorium clapped and laughed at the same time.

Egg went "Woo! Woo!" again.

Madison shrunk into her seat. Running was not an option. Fiona tried to get her to stand up, but she would not budge. It felt like an eternity between the moment Mrs. Wing said her name and the moment the applause and laughter ceased. In that moment Madison Finn realized that maybe—no, *definitely*—she didn't like the spotlight.

Principal Bernard took back the microphone. "So now students will be dismissed in small groups to vote. You will go to Mrs. Wing's class and vote at the computer stations. Do I need to ask this again? Vote nicely—"

Sqweeeeeeeeee.

"And that's all folks!" He pounded the lectern with a happy fist.

Everyone stood up now, waiting for their turn to vote. It was after 2:45 by the time Madison shoved her way out the door of the assembly hall with Fiona. Egg and Drew were walking down the hall in the opposite direction.

"Who are you gonna vote for, Maddie?" Egg teased as he walked by with Drew.

"Uh . . . that's a hard one, Egg," Madison faked. "I just don't know!"

"The site looks good," Egg said. "I admit it."

"Thanks," Madison said.

Fiona smiled at Egg. "Hey, Walter, I mean . . . Egg."

For the first time ever, Egg smiled right back. "Hey, Fiona. Whassup?" He walked away with Drew following closely behind, as usual.

Mrs. Wing's classroom was chaos. People were everywhere.

Some groups of kids were sitting at terminals to punch in their votes while other groups were shuffling around the classroom floor in lines that stretched in a circle.

"Everyone is voting really quickly," Fiona said. "Is that a good sign or a bad sign?"

Madison didn't know. She crossed her fingers inside her pockets just to make sure she was doing everything possible to secure an Aimee victory.

Mrs. Wing saw Madison inside the lab and rushed over to thank her in person. "Well, Madison Finn, we did it. And the voting program seems to be tallying everything up in fine order."

"I'm so glad," Madison mumbled. She was overwhelmed.

Mrs. Wing touched her shoulder. "I am very proud of how hard you worked and how you handled the Web problems, too."

Madison's shoulder drooped into an "Aw, shucks!" pose. She was embarrassed by Mrs. Wing's compliments.

"So, you are staying after school today to help with vote tallies, aren't you?"

Madison nodded.

She would be the first person at Far Hills to know whether or not the election winner would be her worst enemy or her best friend.

What kind of Rude Awakening was in store?

Chapter 14

"It is not possible!" Madison said as she scrolled down the page of election results. They weren't good.

9/21 VOTE TABULATION

Class Seven: 312 students

Ivy Daly	114
Aimee Gillespie	87
Montrell Morris	111
Thomas Kwong	N/A

Not only had Aimee lost to Ivy Daly, but she had come in *third* place after a second-place Montrell Morris.

Ivy had run away with this election. Madison wanted to run away from its results.

The computer automatically did a third vote count to make sure the results were right. It came up the same. Winner: Ivy Daly.

"Mrs. Wing?" Madison asked nicely as could be. "Could I be the one to tell Aimee the bad news about losing?"

Mrs. Wing decided it would be fine on one simple condition. "You can share the news with her tonight, but let's keep the rest of the school in suspense until morning announcements, okay?"

Madison agreed.

The next morning Principal Bernard would get on the announcement speaker to announce all class presidents in grades seven through nine, as well as names of all the vice presidents, class treasurers, and class reps. Madison wanted Aimee to know *before* she heard that announcement.

Aimee had dance practice that day, so Madison didn't get a chance to talk to her alone until after dinnertime. Mrs. Gillespie had made hamburgers, real *meat* ones, in honor of Madison's last night dining and sleeping at their place. It was a full house tonight, with Roger, Billy, Dean, and Doug all home for good eats and good talk about their sister.

"Here's to the next president of Far Hills Junior High." Aimee's dad raised his water glass.

Everyone cheered except for Madison, who gulped her water down and barely spoke.

"Maddie, you're so quiet, what's the problem?"

Aimee asked her when they were waiting for Mrs. Gillespie to bring out dessert.

"Tell ya later," Madison said. She could feel her knee jumping. She was trying to figure out the right time to talk.

It took a few minutes of after-dinner playing with Phin before Madison finally told Aimee.

Aimee grabbed a pillow and screamed into it when she heard the news.

"Aimee?" Madison didn't move. "Aim? Are you okay?"

Slowly, Aimee rolled over to one side. She looked more mad than sad. "Ugh!" she cried out. "She always wins. I can't STAND it!"

"I'm sorry you lost, Aimee, I really am," Madison continued. "And I didn't want to ruin tonight. I just didn't want you to find out at school tomorrow. I wanted to tell you now so you wouldn't be—"

"I know, Maddie," Aimee groaned. "Hey, I tried, right?"

"Yeah," Madison said. "But you deserve it so much more. You really, really, really did."

"Did Ivy really win by that many votes?"

Madison nodded.

"The popular girl always wins, doesn't she?" Aimee grumbled.

Madison thought about that for a moment. She agreed that Ivy seemed to get her way most of the time.

"I think people voted for Ivy because they think they'll be cool or something if she wins."

"Like they'll become a part of her little club or something," Aimee added. "You know, it just makes me so mad!

"I'm gonna go talk to Roger," Aimee sniffled. "Maybe one of my brothers can cheer me up. I am so bummed out. Those guys are always good with this kinda stuff, ya know?"

Madison knew firsthand. Roger gave *great* advice.

As soon as Aimee walked out, Madison started up her orange laptop immediately, hoping to catch Bigwheels online. She needed a big-time mood booster.

The bigfishbowl.com server was a little slow. Too many other people were online at once. When she finally did get on, Madison scrolled down the alphabetical list of people who were in the "fishtank."

```
2good2be2
654aqua
7thheavn4
A+student
Abadabadoo
allurluv
Bethiscool
Bhurley
Bigphat88
Bigwheels
```

She was there! Bigwheels was online! Aimee had lost at school, but here was a smaller victory. Madison felt her stomach flip-flop—but in a *good* way.

INSTA-MESSAGE to Bigwheels
<MadFinn>: R u there?

She waited for only a split second before her answer popped right up.

INSTA-MESSAGE REPLY to MadFinn
<Bigwheels>: MADISON! Meet me in deep sea chat area, ok 4 private chat???
<Bigwheels>: Oh yeah u know my fave room is GOFISHY

Madison was so excited she kept hitting the return key before her message was typed, but she finally got through.

INSTA-MESSAGE REPLY to Bigwheels
<MadFinn>: C
<MadFinn>:
<MadFinn>: SORRY! C u there
<MadFinn>: GOFISHY

Chatting in private was the next-best thing to being right next to someone—and MadFinn and Bigwheels hadn't chatted in a whole week.

<Bigwheels>: S^?
<MadFinn>: election OVER
<Bigwheels>: WHO WON?????????
<MadFinn>: My frind Aimee lost
<MadFinn>: I mean friend
<Bigwheels>: [:>(
<MadFinn>: ı know boohoo
<Bigwheels>: Big smile 2 her
<MadFinn>: 88
<MadFinn>: POAHF
<Bigwheels>: did that other girl win?
<MadFinn>: Yes IVY
<MadFinn>: THAt makes me maddddd
<Bigwheels>: Hey I know an Ivy
<MadFinn>: WHO???
<Bigwheels>: JK
<MadFinn>: LOL
<MadFinn>: I shldnt say stuff rigtht
<Bigwheels>: She could read this
<MadFinn>: Not good to write stuff down like
<MadFinn>: Her name
<Bigwheels>: whatever she wont see
<MadFinn>: Howz school?
<Bigwheels>: RL is no fun
<MadFinn>: I decided to like someone
<Bigwheels>: { :O You did?
<MadFinn>: :>&
<Bigwheels>: STOP Just tell me who is it?

<MadFinn>: Hart
<Bigwheels>: Like HEART? LOL
<MadFinn>: Yeah I guess
<MadFinn>: FC he likes me
<MadFinn>: but I dunno
<Bigwheels>: Is he in ur class?
<MadFinn>: I knew him b4 in 2grade & then he moved but now he's back and he is way dif I dunno no one knows but you so don't tell n e one
<Bigwheels>: LOL who would I tell?
<MadFinn>: oops GMBO
<Bigwheels>: Does he know?
<MadFinn>: He HATES me I think
<Bigwheels>: Do u have classes 2gether?
<MadFinn>: Y r boys so clueless soemtimes?
<Bigwheels>: Boys are annoying
<MadFinn>: u said it!!!
<Bigwheels>: #1 reason: only think of 1 thing
<MadFinn>: what
<Bigwheels>: Hookups
<MadFinn>: Have u ever?
<Bigwheels>: Not xactly
<MadFinn>: 404
<Bigwheels>: Ask the blowfish

"Ask the Blowfish" was a special area on bigfishbowl.com where you could go to ask advice on

matters of the heart and head. It only answered yes and no questions, but Madison swore it was always right.

<Bigwheels>: Hey PAW!!!!
<MadFinn>: what
<Bigwheels>: let's talk tomorrow
<MadFinn>: what
<Bigwheels>: PAW!!
<MadFinn>: ok bye :>)

Madison was about to turn off her computer when she noticed that her mailbox had mail in it.

Fm: Wetwinz
To: MadFinn
Subject: THE ELECTION!
Date: Thurs, 21 Sept., 8:44 PM

Maddie! Chet just told me the worst thing ever I am sooo sad. He says Aimee lost the election. I guess Drew told Egg and Egg told Chet who let the news slip when we had dinner. Oh no what does Aimee think? Please please tell her I am soooo bummed out. I sent an e-m just in case she doesn't know and also I can't get thru on the phone which I can't. I've been trying since 8.

I wanted her to win sooo much. WoW.

Anyway bye.

Madison quickly deleted Fiona's e-mail. She couldn't believe all that had happened in the past week.

Bigwheels had been right about boys. They were so annoying. How could Drew confide in Egg, who had the hugest mouth in all of Far Hills? If Chet knew, that meant that Egg had probably told the rest of the class. Even Ivy probably knew. She would be gloating about her victory before Friday announcements even happened.

But Friday wasn't the drama Madison anticipated. No big surprise that Ivy was her winning self, poisonous as ever.

There was one very important thing that made Friday *very* nice, however, in spite of the election results. Mom had flown in from France that morning, so Madison was going home to her *real* home after school. At *last*.

Madison smelled cloves when she walked through the door. Mom was boiling potpourri and airing out the living room.

"Hello?" Madison said, dumping her orange bag in the front hall. "Are you here, Mom?" She kicked off her sneakers and slid across the wood floor.

Phinnie came running. The Gillespies had

dropped him off already that day, along with all of Madison's overnight bags.

"Rowrooo!" he howled, happy to be back home where he belonged, too.

Mom appeared from behind the kitchen's swinging door, arms outstretched. "Honey bear!" she cried.

Madison squeezed. It felt good to be called that name in person rather than just in e-mail. Mom wrapped her arms around Maddie's middle.

"I missed you!" she said. Madison hugged her even tighter.

Phinnie wanted in on the clinch, too. He jumped up and tried to get Madison's attention as if to say, "Stop holding that human and start hugging ME."

Madison saw a wrapped package on the dining room table with a card: *Je t'aime Madison*.

"That's for you." Mom smiled.

Madison opened the wrapping and saw a wooden box covered with decoupage animals varnished on the surface. She'd never seen anything so beautiful. Inside that box was another surprise: a shiny silver ring with a moonstone top. The band of the ring was little daisies linked together.

"Mom!" Madison burst into happy tears. "I love it. I love it SO much!"

"I thought since your Dad gave you the earrings, this would be a nice match. I picked it up on the Place de la Concorde."

Madison's smile turned downward. "Uh, can we not talk about Dad?"

"Maddie, what is it?" Mom pulled out a kitchen chair. "Is something wrong with your father?"

"No," Madison replied. "Forget it."

"Do you want to talk? Tell me," Mom said. "What is it? Are you upset about Dad's girlfriend?"

Madison didn't answer. Her parents both had a sneaky way of needing to talk and then making it seem like *she* was the one who had something to say.

"You know, I did a lot of thinking while I was away," Mom said, trying to get Madison to talk, too. "I did a lot of thinking about my work and you and—"

Madison stared at the ceiling. She wanted to run, but she stayed put.

"Okay, I get it. You want to talk about this another time." Mom sensed Madison's discomfort and changed the subject. "Are you hungry? Wanna order pizza for dinner? "

"Pizza is perfect!" Madison cheered.

No more sand or soggy vegetable burritos or tofu meatballs.

"Ggggrrrrowrrooooo!" Phin growled. Even the dog was ready to chow down some real food. Mom called in for an extra large pie with extra-cheese.

During dinner, Mom stayed away from the topic of Dad, as requested. But then she started asking

other questions Madison liked even less.

"Why are you asking if I like any boys at school?" Madison said.

"Just curious," Mom replied. "I have been gone a while, honey bear. I don't want to miss anything. Now that you're in seventh grade."

"I don't like *anyone*, Mom," Maddie said firmly.

"Okay." Mom kissed the top of Madison's head. "Okay. I get it. That subject is off-limits too." She went off to clean the dinner dishes.

Of course, Madison *did* like someone. She just didn't want to say his name out loud, not even to Mom, because once it was out there in the universe her chances of getting crushed increased. And she had been crushed enough this week with elections, the Web site and Dad's new girlfriend. Plus, if she said her crush's name out loud, then people would know. Madison wasn't ready for that—or the *Hart* ache. Boy, oh boy.

Mad Chat Words:

[:>(	Serious Frown
:o	Shocked
:>&	Tongue-tied
FTBOMBH	From the Bottom of My Broken Heart
TAL	Thanks a lot
12345	Talk about school
GAL	Get a Life
LMSO	Laughing my socks off
>5	High Five
s>	What's Up?
88	Love and kisses
POAHF	Put on a happy face
JK	Just kidding
404	I have no clue

Madison's Computer Tip:

If you're reading e-mail or surfing the Web and you see something weird, speak up. **Always tell an adult if you see *anything* online that makes you uncomfortable.** Don't be afraid to tell parents or teachers, even if you're embarrassed by it. I had to tell Mrs. Wing, my computer teacher, about the problems with the school site and I was mortified. Safety comes first!

Visit Madison at www.madisonfinn.com

Take a sneak peek at the new

#3: Play It Again

Chapter 1

"I want a dance solo," Aimee Gillepsie announced at lunch. "What about you, Maddie? What part do you wanna get?"

Madison Finn shrugged and took a sip of her chocolate milk.

The Far Hills Junior High administration had decided to organize a special cabaret in honor of the school's assistant principal, Mrs. B. Goode's, twenty years of distinguished service. They were planning three separate nights of entertainment—one for each class in the school. Everyone in the seventh grade was expected to try out for selected scenes and songs from *The Wiz*.

But Madison didn't want to. She couldn't.

Madison couldn't get up onstage to sing some lame rendition of "Happy Birthday" in the key of C.

She couldn't face having other classmates with their eyes fixed on her every onstage move.

And she absolutely couldn't dance.

Just the thought of auditioning made Madison woozier than woozy.

Even worse, Madison couldn't tell her friends that she didn't want to audition, especially her best friend, Aimee. Being afraid is one thing, but having to admit that to other people is another thing.

"Maybe I'll just be one of those creepy trees that talks," Madison finally told Aimee, trying to change the subject. "You know, like on the way to Oz."

"Yeah, Maddie, like that's the part you'd get." Aimee made a face.

"I'm serious," Madison said, flicking her straw at Aimee. Chocolate milk splattered across the orange lunch table.

"Don't get—ahh! My new top!" Aimee cried. The milk just missed her.

She and Madison burst into a goofy fit of laughter.

"Morons," some kid with a buzz cut at the next table grunted. He looked like a ninth grader.

"Takes one to know one," Aimee muttered bravely under her breath.

Madison covered her face with her hands and turned back to the comfort of her lunch: two slices of bread, peanut butter, and a neatly peeled orange

on the side. Orange was Madison's favorite color and her favorite fruit.

"Hello, superstars," Fiona Waters teased, sliding onto the lunch table bench alongside Aimee. Fiona was the new girl in town and at school, and Madison and Aimee were happy to have her as a new part of their group along with their guy friends Walter "Egg" Diaz and his shadow, Drew Maxwell. Fiona's twin brother, Chet, usually hung out with them too.

"Did you check out what Ivy's wearing today?" Fiona whispered.

The three girlfriends twisted their heads to catch a glimpse of Ivy Daly's showy blue-flowered dress.

"That's a Boop-Dee-Doop dress," Aimee sneered. "I saw it in a magazine this month. Figures *she'd* get it."

"She looks good, though, don't you think?" Fiona said.

"Whatever." Aimee's voice bristled.

Once upon a very long time ago, way back in third grade, Madison had been best friends with Ivy, but things had changed a lot over the years. Now Ivy was known as *Poison Ivy*, enemy number one at Far Hills.

Aimee glanced over at the enemy again. "She'll probably get the lead in the play, just like always. She always gets what she wants."

"Uh-huh," Madison agreed, chewing an orange section.

Across the cafeteria, Ivy tossed her red curly hair and looked around the room. No matter how

poisonous she acted, Madison thought, she always managed to get noticed. That was how she won the election for class president and how she won the attention of most boys in the seventh grade. She didn't have to worry about being liked by the popular crowd because Ivy Daly *was* the popular crowd.

"Let's talk about something else, please," Aimee pleaded. "Are you trying out for *The Wiz*, Fiona?"

"Will rehearsals conflict with soccer? I have team practice almost every day after school and—" Fiona paused. "Well, I can't miss soccer. I want to make a good impression with the coach, you know?"

Fiona and Madison had tried out together for the school soccer team, but only Fiona had actually made the team. Fiona had been a soccer star last year when she was living in California, so her making the Far Hills team was no big surprise. And Madison wasn't much of an athlete, so not making the team was no big surprise for her, either. Madison considered it a minor success, actually. She hadn't run away from team tryouts. That was something.

"Do you guys think I can do both at the same time?" Fiona asked.

"Totally," Aimee said. "We're only doing a few scenes, so we won't have rehearsals all the time. Mr. Gibbons schedules them in between normal after-school stuff, I think that's what I heard."

"I want to do both," Fiona said. "I love singing."

"Wait a minute. You play soccer, go to Spanish

club, and you sing, too?" Madison said, a little surprised. She kept learning new things about her new friend. It seemed like Fiona was good at everything she tried to do—and she tried to do a lot. "When do you have time to do homework?"

"In between," Fiona said.

Madison stared down at the table, not saying much. She poured a molehill of sugar onto her lunch tray and traced a path with her fork. She didn't want Aimee to ask questions about the audition.

But it was too late. Aimee reached across the table for Madison's wrist.

"You still haven't said what you're gonna sing at auditions, Maddie!" Aimee cooed.

Before Madison could admit to being all nerves, Egg appeared out of nowhere. He stuck his head in between Aimee and Fiona.

"Are you guys talking about the show?" Egg said.

"Who wants to know?" Aimee growled back.

Egg swiped an apple off her tray and took a big bite. "After tomorrow's audition, everyone can call me *The Wiz*ard."

He put the apple back onto Aimee's tray.

"Wizard? You wish!" Aimee swatted at him. She glanced down at the bitten apple, dripping with his spit. "Soooo gross."

Drew, who was standing there, too, laughed. He stuck his hand up in the air and waved a silent

hello to the rest of the table.

"Drew thinks I have a good shot at the part, so there," Egg said.

Fiona giggled. "You'll probably get the part, Walter," she said softly. "I mean, Egg." She bowed her head, and the beads on her braids clinked. Madison and Aimee both knew that Fiona had a giant, inexplicable crush on him.

Unfortunately, Egg ignored her. Chet had walked up by now, and the three boys sat down in a cluster at the other end of the table.

"Whassup?" Chet mumbled.

"We're talking about auditions for *The Wiz*," Fiona said.

"Yeah," Madison jumped in. "Egg thinks he can be cast as—"

"A Munchkin," Aimee interrupted. "And I think that's a safe bet."

Chet cracked up. "Hey, fool! She got you."

Egg smirked. "And I'll get her back—when she least expects it."

"Well, I don't know what you guys are doing, but we're *all* trying out for the play tomorrow," Aimee said as she pointed to herself, Fiona, and Madison.

Madison leaned across the table, whispering, "Aimee, I'm not sure that I want to—"

The bell rang for the next period. In an instant the group dumped their trays, grabbed their books, and exited the cafeteria doors. Madison almost

bumped into Ivy as they left the lunchroom.

"Ex-cuse me," Ivy said. "Watch it."

Her annoying drones, Rose Thorn and Phony Joanie, followed close behind, pushing past Madison, too. They always traveled in a pack.

A rat pack, Madison thought as they scampered away.

Later that night, Madison asked her mom what she should do about *The Wiz*. She hoped Mom had the instant cure for all this audition anxiety, like how she poured eucalyptus oil in the bathtub when Madison had a cold.

"Gee, honey bear," Mom said gently, tickling her daughter's back. "No one says you have to audition."

"I have to be a part of the show, Mom." Madison sighed. "I can't just sit back and be scenery. I'm in junior high now."

"It could be a lot of fun. . . ."

"What's so *fun* about standing onstage while everyone and their parents stare at me?"

"William Shakespeare says, 'The play's the thing,'" Mom said. She paused. "You know who William Shakespeare is, right?"

"No duh, Mom. We read *Romeo and Juliet*, remember? Geesh. "

"Rowrooooo!" Madison's dog, Phin, agreed.

The pug rushed over toward them, tail wagging in excited circles. His whole butt jerked as he huffed and puffed.

"Good doggie," Madison said as she bent down. Phinnie licked her chin. "What do *you* think I should do?" she asked him sweetly.

Mom came up with another suggestion. "If you don't want to act or sing, then why not try something else to help the show? You don't want to be a part of the scenery, but you could *paint* the scenery, right? You could paint a castle or something. Is there a castle in *The Wiz*?"

"I think." Madison shrugged.

"Well." Mom reached out to hug her daughter. "I know whatever you decide to do, it'll be great."

Before bed that night, Madison and Phin curled up in bed with her laptop computer. She punched in her secret password and opened a brand-new file.

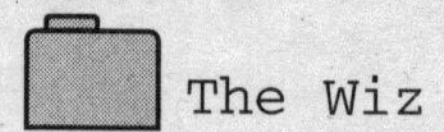

Rude Awakening: The play is definitely not the thing. I don't care what William Shakespeare says.

Or what Mom says.

Tomorrow they're holding auditions and tomorrow I am doomed. And of course Aimee won't understand when I tell her I can't try out. She'll say I'm just being chicken. It's so easy for her. And Fiona, too, obviously. Who knew that she could play soccer, look great, *and* sing? Well, she can. No one will understand why I'm so scared to try.

I remember one time when I had to sing Christmas carols onstage at school and I passed out, fell right there on the floor like a lump. Some teacher in a Santa suit had to carry me out of the assembly and everyone was staring.

What if that happens again? What if I faint—or worse, throw up—in front of the world?

What if *Hart Jones* sees me do that?

The whole time Hart followed me around in second grade he was SUCH a pest. Now why do I feel like following him? I saw him today in the hall when we left science class. I pray he didn't notice me staring.

If he tries out, I really think I should try out.

I need to call Dad. He'll know what to do.

From the Files of
Madison Finn